THE
FINAL NIGHTMARE

Look for all the books in the
HOUSE ON CHERRY STREET
trilogy:

THE
HOUSE
ON
CHERRY
STREET

THE
FINAL NIGHTMARE
BOOK III

**RODMAN PHILBRICK
AND LYNN HARNETT**

AN
APPLE
PAPERBACK

SCHOLASTIC INC.
New York Toronto London Auckland Sydney

For Moira, Miranda, Molly, and Annie

ISBN 0-590-25515-0

12 11 10 9 8 7 6 5 4 3 2   5 6 7 8 9/9 0/0

Printed in the U.S.A.   40

First Scholastic printing, August 1995

1

My sister and I were alone. Really alone.

And something inside the house on Cherry Street wanted to hurt us, just like it had hurt the baby-sitter.

"Jay-sonnnnn! Jason come here!"

That was Sally, my four-year-old sister. Sally was outside, watching the ambulance take the baby-sitter away after she'd fallen and gotten knocked out.

I'd gone back into the house — a house I knew was haunted — to call my parents. I wasn't going to tell them about the ghost because they'd never believe me.

In as calm a voice as possible I was going to ask my parents to come right home. Come home before it was too late.

But the phone number was gone. I had no idea how to reach them.

"That's it," I said to myself. "I've got to get us out of here."

I headed for the front door, determined not to spend another moment in that creepy old house. No way.

Just as I got to the door, the lock snapped shut!

Eerie laughter echoed from inside the walls. Laughter of a witch who'd been dead for a hundred years. Laughter from an empty tomb.

I pounded my fist on the door. It was no use — the house had taken me prisoner.

"*Jayyy-sssssssonnnnnnn!*" something whispered from the dark.

It wasn't my sister's voice. It wasn't the voice of anything alive.

"Get out!" I shouted. "Get out of this house and leave us alone!"

Who was I kidding? You can't scare a ghost away by shouting. The thing was here to stay — and now it wanted to keep me here forever, too.

Maybe someday *I'd* be the ghost in the walls. Maybe *I'd* be the spirit who wandered around at night, repeating the moment of my death.

I shuddered at the thought — I had to get out before the creeping fear drove me crazy.

"Jason, come quick!"

That was Sally, calling from outside. It sounded like she was in trouble.

I raced to a window, but it slammed shut just as I got there.

Then something moved behind me. I whirled

2

around, but all I could see were shadows. Dark, murky shadows reaching out to touch me.

I closed my eyes. "Get a grip," I told myself. "Your eyes are playing tricks again."

But when I opened my eyes, something *was* reaching for me.

"Jason!"

A hand came out of the darkness and grabbed me.

2

It was my sister. Standing there tugging on my arm as she looked up at me.

"How'd you get in here?" I demanded.

"I walked in the door, silly," she said.

I looked and saw moonlight coming in through the open door. And just a minute before it had been locked.

"Come on," I said, grabbing Sally's hand. "We're getting out of here!"

I expected the door to slam shut just as we got there, but it didn't. It was like the house had decided to let us go for the time being.

As we ran down the driveway, away from the house, I looked back. Expecting to see a small, ghostly face in the window. The face of the little boy who'd died there a long time ago.

But the windows were empty. Like a row of broken glass eyes, as dark as the shadows that lurked inside the house.

"Come on," Sally said, urging me on. "They're almost here!"

"What are you talking about?"

"Mom and Dad," she said. "They're coming back."

I took hold of Sally and stopped her in her tracks. "Hang on," I said. "Don't get your hopes up. Mom and Dad aren't due back until the end of the week."

Sally shook her head and stamped her feet. A sure sign that she was about to have a temper tantrum. For once in my life I couldn't blame her — she'd been awake all night, running from the spirits that had taken over the house. And with the baby-sitter gone she wanted her mommy back, just like any four-year-old.

"Sally, listen to me," I said. "We'll be okay. We'll go over to the neighbor's house and use the phone from there."

The moonlight was fading from the night sky. Soon it would be morning — maybe things would look better in the light of day. But Sally wasn't in the mood to wait.

"They're coming, Jason. Bobby *told* me they're coming."

Bobby told her. Great. Bobby was the little boy who'd died in the house. Bobby was a ghost. Bobby was scary but he wasn't bad really. Just confused. And lonely. He wanted Sally to stay with him — even if she had to become a ghost too.

Unfortunately, Bobby wasn't the only ghost. There was an evil witch who hated everything, especially children, even dead children like Bobby. And this horrible house wanted to kill me and Sally. I knew now that only ghosts could live here.

Of course my parents didn't believe in ghosts — they thought Bobby was an "invisible friend" my sister had invented. They never heard the phantom voices or saw the skeleton creature that came out of the dark when you least expected it. They blamed it on my overactive imagination, or bad dreams, or the usual creaks and groans peculiar to an old house. And so they had gone away on a business trip, leaving my sister and me with Katie, a teenaged baby-sitter.

Katie hadn't believed in ghosts, either. Not at first. But now she knew better. Better than to ever return to the house on Cherry Street.

"Mommy!" Sally cried. "Daddy!"

She let go of my hand and ran away before I could stop her. I shouted but she kept going, disappearing into the row of tall, shadowy pines that surrounded the house and hid it from the main road.

"Wait for me!"

I took off as fast as I could, but slipped and fell on the slick pine needles. WHAM! I landed hard enough to knock the wind out of me.

When I got my breath back I'd lost sight of my little sister.

"Sally," I called out. "Come back!"

But there was no answer. Could that evil old witch-thing be chasing her? Sally wouldn't run from little Bobby. She didn't know anything about ghosts. She thought Bobby was her friend.

Sally didn't understand how he wanted her to be his friend forever — to be a ghost like him.

I almost reached the road before I caught sight of Sally again.

She was jumping up and down at the side of the driveway in her pajamas, clutching her stuffed bunny and shouting, "Mommy! Mommy!" over and over.

Dropping down beside her, I said, "Sally, you shouldn't run from me like that."

"But Mommy and Daddy are coming," said Sally, pointing down the road. "I saw them."

Saw them? Impossible.

"You couldn't have, Sally," I said. "You can't see the road from the yard."

But Sally kept bouncing up and down, looking down the road like she expected Mom and Dad to drive up any second.

Well, at least we were away from the house. The sun was high enough now so it almost cleared the tops of the trees. In a little while we could go to Steve's house and use the phone.

Steve's family spent summers in the house next door. He'd help me figure out what to do.

Then I saw a glint of metal as a car rounded a bend in the road. My heart skipped a beat.

Hardly anybody drove down here. There was nothing at the end of Cherry Street but the lake. The only houses were a few summer cottages and our gabled old monstrosity.

I caught another glimpse of the car. This time there was no doubt. It was definitely our family station wagon! I wanted to leap for joy like Sally.

Then I remembered. The house was a total wreck. Our baby-sitter was in the hospital. And Mom and Dad didn't believe in ghosts.

How was I going to explain it all?

3

"**J**ason! Sally!"

The car jolted to a stop. My dad had the window rolled down and he was leaning out and grinning at us.

"The job got through sooner than we expected," he said. "How did you know we were coming?"

"What a nice surprise!" said my mom, getting out of the car. Then suddenly her smile faded and was replaced by a look of concern. "What's Sally doing in her pajamas and no shoes?"

Dad checked out Sally and frowned. "You've got some explaining to do, Jay. And now that I think of it, where's the baby-sitter? Don't tell me you sneaked out here without telling her."

"Um," I said. "Yeah, well, you see . . ."

How was I going to tell them that a ghost had injured our baby-sitter?

"Bobby was in trouble," said Sally helpfully. "Katie hit her head."

"What!"

"Ah, what happened is, Katie got hurt," I said uneasily. "I had to call an ambulance. They took her to the hospital."

"When? How badly is she injured?" Dad asked urgently.

"Do her parents know?" asked Mom.

"Pretty bad," I said. "She was unconscious. It just happened. I couldn't call anybody because, um, the phone is out of order."

Mom and Dad looked at each other, horrified.

"But, Jason, what happened?" demanded Mom.

I tried to explain but Mom and Dad just looked more bewildered and upset.

"Get in the car," said Dad finally. "We'll check with the hospital, Carol. Then we'll fetch Katie's parents and go see how she is."

I was so relieved to have them home I almost forgot about what a wreck the house was until I was settled in the backseat headed up the driveway.

Should I try now to explain? No time. Besides, they wouldn't believe me until they saw it for themselves. I'd tell them everything as soon as we got to the house. At least now they'd have to admit I wasn't making it up about the ghosts.

As we drove under the pines, sunlight glinted off the windows of the house — just exactly like the first day we'd arrived.

But wait! The house didn't have any glass in the windows. They'd all blown in last night! Every one of them!

But now each pane was smooth and perfect, sparkling in the early morning sunshine.

4

Mom and Dad hurried toward the house while
I hung back, getting their suitcase out of
the car. Sally put her hand in mine as Mom and
Dad climbed the porch stairs.

I braced myself. Mom had the front door open.
Any second now she would let out a yell when she
saw all the furniture and antiques that had been
smashed up during the night of horror.

Mom disappeared inside. Dad, too. They didn't
make a sound.

Sally and I looked at each other.

"Bobby fixed it," she said. "He fixed everything, even the phone."

"Not this time," I said. "No way. It was like a
bomb went off in there."

"You'll see," she said, smiling secretly.

We went up the porch and into the house and
stopped in the broad front hallway.

Everything was back in its place.

The living room couch and chairs had been

moved back to where they belonged around that ugly, barf-colored rug my mother liked so much. The tinkly lamps were back on their tables, the broken vases and candlesticks and china figures were back on their shelves, perfectly whole.

I shouldn't have been surprised. It had happened once before. At night during the worst of the haunting the air was thick with flying objects exploding into smithereens against the wall or ceiling or floor. Then in the morning it was like nothing had happened.

But I thought this time it would be different. This time Katie had been hurt — the house had tried to kill us, not just scare us away. For me that changed things.

But not for the ghosts who roamed the house on Cherry Street. Now I knew they didn't care who they hurt or how badly.

Sally gripped my hand tightly. "Maybe Katie's head is all better," she said, looking around at the rooms she had last seen littered with broken glass and overturned furniture.

"No, Sally, she's not all better," I said, kneeling down in front of her. I pushed up my sleeve to show Sally the cut I'd gotten last night from flying glass. It wasn't a big cut, but it hadn't magically disappeared, either. "People don't go back together like chairs and lamps. When people get hurt, they stay hurt."

Sally's lower lip trembled.

I felt bad but I had to try to make Sally understand the danger. The ghosts were already dead. Why should they care what happened to living people?

Sally and I followed the sound of voices into the kitchen. Mom was on the phone to the hospital. She looked pale and worried.

"Thank God," she said when she hung up the phone. "They said Katie will be okay. Her parents are already at the hospital."

Relief made my knees turn rubbery. And for some strange reason my stomach felt swirly, like I was going to throw up.

"Jay?" Dad asked. "Are you okay?"

I nodded and took a deep breath.

"You're both exhausted," Mom said. "Why don't you guys take a quick nap while your father and I finish unpacking? We'll wake you up in an hour or so and we'll all have a big breakfast. How does that sound?"

"Sounds good, Mom," I said, yawning. She was right. I *was* exhausted.

I walked my little sister upstairs and put her to bed. She hugged her stuffed bunny and was asleep before her head hit the pillow.

Out in the hallway I was heading for my bedroom when a door creaked open behind me.

I turned. The attic door had swung open. A cool breeze came down the attic stairs.

Forget it, Jason, I told myself. Go to bed.

But something drew me to that attic door. Why was a breeze coming down from up there? I had to find out.

My feet made not a sound on the steps. Not even a creak.

Sunlight shone yellow through the opening at the top of the stairs. I could see dust hanging thick in the air like a misty curtain.

I stepped into the attic.

I gasped in surprise. And instantly bent over coughing as the dust flowed down my throat. But I didn't care.

The attic was a wreck!

The walls were totally smashed in. There were big holes in the floor.

And Bobby's rocking chair was still there!

The little rocking chair was the only thing that wasn't smashed to bits — everything else was broken or damaged.

Even my parents would have to believe the house was really haunted when they saw this!

I was about to yell for my dad. Then I heard something move behind me. A rustling, sneaky sound in the shadows.

The back of my neck tingled.

I was slowly turning around to look when a horrible voice spoke right by my ear. A creaky, raspy voice of the undead.

"You!" it shrieked. *"It's all your fault! I'll get you! I'll get you for good!"*

15

I spun around. My heart leaped into my throat.

The witch-thing was there, eyes glowing from inside her black cloak. The same creature who haunted the place in the dark.

"ARGGGGHHHHH!"

It charged straight for me, snarling.

I was frozen to the spot.

Her eyes burned with fury.

One gnarled claw reached for my throat. In the other she held the sledgehammer. The same hammer that had smashed these walls to bits.

She cackled. Her black eyes glittered with vengeful glee.

I couldn't move.

Cold, bony fingers closed around my neck.

The last thing I saw was the blur of the sledgehammer. Then the world went black.

5

Everything hurt. I was afraid to open my eyes and look.

I strained my ears. Was the witch-thing still there? I couldn't hear a thing.

But I felt her crouching over me, waiting. As soon as I opened my eyes she would pounce.

I lay there for what seemed like forever. My nose began to itch. Then my knee. I tried to work out a plan but the itching filled my whole head. I had to move.

Very carefully I opened my eyes a slit. No witch. I moved my head an inch. Nobody there.

I blew out my breath and jumped up, scratching all over.

Ouch!

She must have really knocked me with that sledgehammer. I hurt in places I didn't know I had.

But she hadn't killed me, even though I knew I had seen murder in her eyes. Maybe she was weaker in the daytime. Yes, that was probably it! The sun sapped her strength.

I hobbled toward the door, working out a new plan in my head. A way to stop the haunting!

Then I heard a thud downstairs. And another.

The floor began to shake with the force of these new blows. Was the witch-thing taking her sledgehammer to the living room?

I was tempted to stay hidden up here until the noise stopped. But whatever was happening downstairs, Mom and Dad would think I was responsible.

I had to try to stop it.

Before I could change my mind, I left the attic. Pausing in the second floor hallway, I couldn't hear anything breaking. No crunches or splinterings or tinkling of glass.

Just BANG! BANG! BANG!

I crept down the stairs to the first floor. There was no one in the living room or the dining room. The sound was coming from the back of the house.

The basement!

My feet pulled me along the hallway to the kitchen. My mind was blank — it was as if I'd lost control of my body.

The pounding got louder.

But it wasn't the basement door that was dancing in its frame. It was the kitchen door. The furious banging was coming from outside.

18

As I stood stuck to the spot, the doorknob began to turn.

I stared at it in horror.

Was it Bobby, the dead boy? Or the witch-thing coming to get me?

The door shook and bulged.

A voice from the grave shouted out my name. *"Jayyy-son! Jayyy-son!"*

The door swung open.

6

A big dark shape filled the doorway, blotting out the sun.

"Jason? Is that you?"

I turned to jelly with relief. It was only Steve, my bud from next door.

"What's going on?" he asked. "How come your parents are back already?"

I shrugged. "The job didn't take as long as they thought, that's all."

"Yeah?" He sounded doubtful. "What was all the fuss over here late last night? I thought I heard screaming."

"Must have been the ambulance siren," I said, acting casual. Like it was no big deal.

"The ambulance? Cool! What happened?"

As I told Steve about our horrible night, with the ghosts chasing us up into the attic and out onto the roof, his eyes got bigger and bigger.

"You're making it up," he said. "The baby-sitter really broke her arm?"

I nodded. "She's okay now."

"So you guys were left here on your own?"

"Only for a little while," I said. "Then my parents came back. The witch-thing is still here, though. She just came after me with a sledgehammer. I'm lucky to be alive."

Steve was kind of staring at me, trying to figure out if I was telling the truth. He's a big, athletic kid, a star pitcher for his baseball team, and a real practical joker. He was always pulling some prank or another, but he'd seen enough of the haunting himself to know I wasn't making it up.

"Any grub in this joint?" he asked, switching his attention to the cookie jar.

"Help yourself," I said.

Steve thoughtfully munched an Oreo and gave me a quizzical look. "You really got attacked with a sledgehammer?"

I pointed to the bruise on my forehead.

"I thought the ghosts only came out at night," he said.

"That's what I thought, too."

He sighed and wiped crumbs from his mouth. "Totally weird," he said.

Just then my mom came into the kitchen. "Hello, Steve," she said. "I see you boys found the cookies."

"Hi, Mrs. Winter," he said. "Welcome back."

"Jay, I just got off the phone with Katie's mother," Mom said. "Your father and I feel responsible for what happened to her."

"It wasn't your fault," I said.

"Nevertheless, she was in our house. We're going over to the hospital to make sure she's okay. Will you and your sister be okay for an hour or so?"

"Sure, Mom."

"Sally's still sound asleep. So I don't want a lot of horsing around in here," she said, eyeing Steve.

"No problemo," I said.

A couple of minutes later the station wagon was heading back down the driveway. Steve and I watched it go.

"What do we do now?" he asked. "You want to play ball? Or we could go swimming."

"I can't leave Sally alone," I said.

"But she's asleep," he protested.

"You know better than that," I said. "But I do have something in mind."

"Yeah? Like what?"

"Like an expedition."

Steve grinned. "Right. Like to the North Pole, right?"

"Worse," I said. "To the basement."

"The basement?" he said, looking puzzled. "Why?"

"Because there's something down there I want to find."

Steve raised his eyebrows. "Like what?" he asked.

"A body," I said. "A dead body."

7

It was Steve's idea to call up Lucy. She's about our age, with long dark hair and a very serious expression — except when she smiles. Lucy knows all about the haunting.

All in all she's pretty cool for a girl.

"Lucy was the one who told us about how they never found the old lady's body," Steve reminded me.

It was true. Lucy had a lot of good ideas about why there were ghosts on Cherry Street and I thought she secretly wanted to see them for herself.

She showed up right away, her eyes glowing with excitement, and I told her my idea about searching for the missing body.

"I don't see what we can do against a ghost," said Lucy doubtfully. "We're only human."

I ignored that. "It's the witch-thing that's doing the really bad stuff," I said. "And the basement

24

is her territory. I can feel her down there. Steve thinks it might be the ghost of the old lady."

"Right," said Steve. "If we find her body and give it a decent burial, maybe she'll go away."

Lucy shuddered. "What about the other ghost?" she asked. "The little boy?"

I took a deep breath. "I think he's been trying to protect us from the bad ghost. But he's not powerful enough."

"The whole idea gives me the creeps," Lucy said.

"We don't have any choice," I insisted. "We've got to do something."

"Okay," said Lucy reluctantly. "What's the plan?"

"We go into the basement, find her — or her body — and drag it out."

"But how do you know the body's in the basement?" asked Lucy.

I'd been thinking about that for quite a while, and I thought I finally had the answer.

"Because that's the one place Bobby never goes," I said. "That's how."

8

Steve and Lucy went back home to get ready for the expedition into the haunted basement. We agreed to meet at my house in a half hour.

It didn't take me long to get ready. All I needed was my flashlight, an extra battery, a stick for poking into corners, and a long, thick rope.

Then I sat around waiting, trying not to look at the clock every thirty seconds.

But Steve and Lucy were right on time. Both of them had changed from shorts into long pants. Lucy wore overalls with pockets everywhere, all of them bulging with stuff.

"I brought a flashlight," she said, "and a Swiss army knife. If we find a coffin we can pry open the lid with it. I've got a screwdriver, too."

Steve was wearing some kind of lumpy necklace.

Lucy squinted at it. "Is that garlic?"

Steve shrugged. "Yeah. Just in case."

"That's to keep away vampires," I said. "I don't think it'll work on ghosts."

"Phew!" Lucy laughed. "It'll keep me away, that's for sure."

"What's that for?" asked Steve, pointing at the rope slung over the back of a kitchen chair.

"I thought we should rope ourselves together like mountain climbers do," I said. "So we won't get separated."

"So one of us won't get snatched away, is what you really mean," said Lucy. "Good idea."

"Come on," I said, uncoiling the rope. "Let's get going."

I tied the rope around my waist then passed it to Lucy who did the same.

Steve looked doubtful. "Well, if I fall into the witch's bubbling cauldron of slime," he joked, "at least I know you guys will be coming after me, one way or the other."

I led the way to the basement door. My heart was booming in my chest. "Are you ready?" I asked.

"Go for it," Steve said. But his voice cracked.

"Here goes nothing," I said.

I pushed the door to the basement. As it swung open the creaking noise went right up my spine.

"We could always do this tomorrow," Steve said suddenly. "Yeah, tomorrow would be perfect."

Lucy rolled her eyes. "Let's get it over with."

I peered cautiously into the basement. It sure was dark down there — I couldn't see anything but dim shadows and formless shapes.

"Well," said Steve, trying to sound tough. "What are we waiting for?"

I propped a kitchen chair against the basement door. "So the door can't lock behind us," I explained.

"Excellent," said Steve. But he didn't sound convinced.

We turned to face the darkness at the top of the stairs.

From down in the basement I heard a PLOP, like something diving below the surface of a thick liquid. Which was ridiculous. There was no water down there, not even a puddle.

"Did you hear that?" Steve whispered. "Sounds like dripping blood."

Lucy groaned. "You guys are being stupid," she said. "Let just do it."

So we did.

I flipped on the light switch.

The only light came from a bare bulb hanging by a wire from the ceiling at the bottom of the stairs.

Lucy and Steve crowded behind me to look. The light was so dim we could barely make out the stairs. They were dusty and sagged in the middle.

"What's that smell?" asked Lucy in a hushed voice.

A peculiar odor rose up at us. It smelled like dirty socks and moldy bread and wet garbage. It smelled like air that had been shut up with dead things for a long time.

"Rat turds," said Steve. "There are definitely rats down there."

I scowled at him. "It's just the dirt floor," I told Lucy. "The house is so old the basement doesn't have a cement floor."

"It smells old all right," said Lucy. "Like a mummy might come lurching up the stairs at us any second."

"What's that dripping noise?" asked Steve.

"Dripping?" I echoed, stalling. "I didn't hear any dripping." It wasn't a lie, really. What I'd heard sounded more like some scaly finned creature dropping into slimy depths.

I started down.

PLOP!

"I hear it!" said Lucy breathlessly.

"Must be a leaky pipe," I said, but I didn't move. "No big deal."

"Did you ever see *Alien*?" Steve said. "The part where the creature is hiding up in the shadows and all they can hear is the drip-drip-drip of its slimy saliva?"

My determination was slipping away. My stomach felt queasy.

"That was just a movie!" scoffed Lucy. "It's probably just a leaky pipe or something."

She nudged my back. "We'd better check it out," she insisted. "A leaky pipe could make a big mess and you said there's lots of valuable old stuff down there."

So I took a deep breath and started down the stairs with my friends close behind. My ankles tingled as if something under the stairs was itching to grab them. Every time I set my foot down on a tread I half expected claws to sink into my ankles.

When I couldn't stand it another second, I crouched down and swept my flashlight beam over the dark space under the stairs.

Steve jumped. Shadows shrank from the light.

"What?" cried Lucy.

There was nothing there.

I let out a breath. "Just being careful," I said, my voice sounding too loud, as if something was listening down below.

I went down a couple more steps. We were more than halfway.

The light from the bare bulb stuck close to the stairs, like it was afraid to venture out into the basement. I strained my eyes to see beyond it but the blackness was like a solid thing.

Anything could be watching us, cloaked in the dark, invisible.

All I could see were humped shapes. Was something lurking among the stacks of boxes and broken furniture? Waiting for us?

Then it happened.

"Screeee-screee-screeeeeee!"

Something hurtled up out of the dark. A blur of motion, it flew flapping and screaming straight at us.

Steve screamed as it hit his face. He fell, giving the rope a sharp tug.

Lucy's arms pinwheeled as she struggled to keep her balance and failed.

The rope yanked me.

I grabbed for the railing but the flapping thing blinded me. It beat at my face, trying to get at my eyes. I threw my hands up in front of me and lost my balance.

I went down hard in the dark, the creature shrieking above me.

9

We were a tangle of legs and rope.
        I kicked the coils of rope off me, rubbing my back where I'd fallen.

"I hate bats," said Steve, hunching his shoulders around his ears and darting his eyes around, looking for it.

"It wasn't a bat, silly," said Lucy. "It was just a poor terrified bird. A robin, I think."

My heart whacked against my ribs.

A bird, that was all. And I'd thought it was going to pop out my eyeballs and slurp them down whole.

The three of us got shakily to our feet.

"Where did it go?" I asked.

"It think it flew upstairs," said Lucy. "How did it get in?"

"Yeah," said Steve. "All the basement windows are boarded up."

I shrugged. "One of the boards must have come loose."

"Yeah?" said Steve. "Maybe something pried the boards loose, you ever think of that?"

"As a matter of fact, I did," I said. "That's why we're down here, remember? To end the haunting, one way or another."

PLOP! PING!

"What's that?" Lucy said in a hushed voice.

It was the sound of fat, slimy worms dropping from the ceiling into a pit of goo.

We looked at each other. Steve was clutching the banister tightly. Lucy's brown eyes looked like black holes.

We started down again.

At the bottom Lucy switched her flashlight on. Big humps rose up out of the dark and settled into the light beam as torn sofas, stacks of boxes, broken chairs.

"Sure is dark down here," she said. "I don't know when I've seen so much junk all in one place. I bet there's a lot of great stuff here."

"You could hide a body down here and no one would find it for a hundred years," said Steve, his voice cracking.

I shivered. "Let's start over there," I said, pointing with my flashlight.

"And what if we find the body?" asked Lucy, the beam wavering in her hand.

"We bring it upstairs into the light," I said, feeling a little sick at the thought. "Ghosts can't stand the light. It'll rob her of all her powers. And then my parents can give her a decent funeral."

Something slithered in the dark.

"What was that?" cried Lucy, jerking her flashlight around.

PLOP! DRIP!

Startled, she swung her light the other way. We both aimed our beams at the sound.

A long, skinny, black snake hung and writhed from the ceiling beam.

"There it is!" cried Steve. "Somebody's already put a bucket under it."

I blinked and the snake became just an old electrical cord left slung over the rafter.

There was a bucket on the floor under a pipe with a slow drip. I felt my racketing heart slow down a little.

But wait! Who had put that bucket there? Not my dad. He had been gone for days. I was sure the bucket hadn't been there the last time I was down here.

I was pretty sure.

"Let's get started," said Lucy. "This place gives me the creeps."

"Oh, yeah?" jeered Steve. "And what if we find a rotting old skeleton? What's that going to give you? The heebie-jeebies?"

Lucy snugged the rope knot at her waist. "I don't think there's a body down here," she said. "For one thing, it would smell."

"Not if it was a skeleton," said Steve. "Besides,

if you don't think there's a body, what are you doing here?"

"There might be something else," said Lucy. "A clue. We'll know it when we see it."

I didn't say anything. The basement did smell. It smelled like something had been dead and rotting down here for a long time. And the smell was getting stronger.

"I want to start over here," I said. "There's a trunk I want to check out — "

Lucy let out a bloodcurdling scream. Her flashlight dropped to the floor and rolled away.

She backed into me, jabbering, and I fell over a box.

The flashlight flew out of my hands.

It bounced on the floor and went out.

We were in total darkness.

10

"I saw it!" screamed Lucy. "It's coming for us. It has no head!"

Steve's laughter rang out, bouncing off the stone walls.

He scooped up Lucy's flashlight and aimed it over her head.

A headless, armless creature loomed at us out of the dark. I could see how it looked to Lucy.

"It's a dressmaker's dummy, dummy," said Steve, howling with glee.

I got up off the floor and felt around for my flashlight. "You were pretty spooked yourself the first time you saw it," I reminded Steve.

"That was then," he said, grinning. "It'll take more than a dummy to scare me now."

Lucy grabbed her flashlight and took a closer look at the thing, a life-size figure of a woman, made for fitting clothes. "You should have warned me," she said in an injured tone.

I shook my flashlight and, amazingly, it came

on. I pointed it toward the dummy. "Steve and I found a trunk last time we were down here," I said, scanning the area with my light. "But I don't see — there it is!"

The trunk — a big one, big enough to hold the dressmaker's dummy, or a body — was farther back than I remembered. There were a lot of boxes in front of it.

"Help me move this stuff out of the way," I said. "I have a feeling about that trunk. There were some letters in it, but when I came back to look for them they were gone. Maybe they fell behind it or under it or something. Help me look."

"We already looked in there," Steve said, sounding irritated.

"Steve, you're not scared, are you?" Lucy taunted him, flashing a grin at me.

We all froze at a slithering noise. It was coming from behind all the piles of junk.

"That's the noise I heard before," whispered Lucy.

"Mice," I said, not at all sure.

"It's too big to be mice," said Steve uncertainly. "Maybe it's a cat. Maybe it came in after that bird."

The slithering became a scratching.

As if something with long claws was sharpening them on the stone walls.

We backed up a little and huddled closer together. I shone my flashlight toward the sound but couldn't see anything. My knees felt rubbery.

"Here, kitty, kitty," called Lucy in a faint, squeaky voice.

The scratching stopped. I felt Lucy and Steve stiffen on either side of me.

It was watching us. Watching us from the dark.

Then came a low hissing noise, and something heavy slid toward us across the floor.

We took another step back. Our muscles were so rigid we were like statues roped together.

I turned to whisper — I was going to suggest going upstairs, just for a minute, to find some more lights, get a drink of water, anything to get out of here — but I didn't get the chance.

The snake-hiss noise got louder. It snarled.

The thing in the dark was angry.

Suddenly a cardboard box came flying out of the corner. It landed with a heavy thud.

Whatever kicked it was mad. And strong.

"I don't think that was a cat," whispered Lucy.

"Definitely not a cat," Steve agreed.

No, it wasn't a cat. But if it wasn't a cat, what was it?

I didn't really want to stick around to find out.

But when I looked back at the stairs I saw the box had landed right between us and our most direct route out.

I looked at the box. Was there something moving inside it?

Something struggling to get out?

11

"**J**ason! Look!" Steve gripped my arm.

Lucy gasped.

I didn't want to look away from the box. I had it fixed in my mind that if I looked away, small creatures with needle-sharp teeth would spill out and disappear into the shadows, ready to cut our ankles to ribbons when we attempted to escape up the stairs.

"Jason!" Steve's voice cracked. His fingers dug into my shoulder.

I tore my eyes from the box.

At first I almost didn't see it. It was a black shape in the darkness, a shadow among all the other shadows.

But it moved. It slithered along the wall around the edges of the basement.

Gliding through the shadows as if all the piles of junk in its way didn't even exist.

And its glowing eyes were fixed on us.

The thing in the shadows was circling us.

"If we don't get out of here right now," Steve whispered, "I'm going to wet my pants."

We took a step backward, toward the stairs, then another.

The thing bared sharp teeth and hissed in fury.

It started moving faster.

Then it disappeared.

It wasn't there.

We gripped one another.

One thing we knew — it wasn't gone. We couldn't see it, but it definitely could see us. We could feel the evil eyes probing from the dark.

We ran for the stairs.

"AHHHHHHHHHH!"

With a shriek, the thing sprang from the shadows and rushed at us, skeleton hands outstretched.

It was the witch-thing! And her weird eyes were locked on mine. I could feel the hate radiate from her. The creature hated anything alive.

It reached for my neck, clawed fingers twitching.

The creature's foul breath stunned me like a poison cloud.

The last thing I breathed as it started to choke the life out of me was that rotten, garbage-smelling breath.

12

Something grabbed my waist and jerked me hard out of the witch's grasp.

I stumbled and heard someone shouting from a long ways off.

"Jason! Quick! Run!"

The witch's screech of fury blasted me with her poisonous breath. I felt like I was drowning in a sewer.

My sight dimmed.

Icy finger bones scrabbled at my collar, reaching for my neck.

I felt another sharp tug at my waist.

"Jason! Come on!"

Lucy was pulling desperately on the rope that tied the three of us together, yanking us toward the stairs.

Steve grabbed my arm and I shook my head to get rid of the foul-smelling fog that surrounded me.

"You're mine!" shrieked the witch. *"Mine!"*

I tripped over a box and fell down. I felt her hot breath blister my neck.

Something rattled in the box and I rolled away, panicked with a vision of hundreds of razor-sharp teeth.

The witch cackled in triumph as her fingers dug into my shoulder.

She started to drag me back into the shadows of the basement.

I knew I was a goner.

Then Lucy grabbed the box and heaved it. Missing my head, it connected with the thing behind me.

There was a cry of pain and I was free.

"Take that you — you — you old witch!" Lucy shouted.

Steve jerked me to my feet and Lucy charged for the stairs, pulling us along behind her.

I stumbled again at the bottom of the stairs but Lucy kept going, tugging on the rope while Steve pushed me from behind.

We fell into the kitchen, our chests heaving with exhaustion.

I slammed the door behind us and bolted it.

"I can't believe I really saw it," said Lucy, getting her breath back. "It was even more horrible than you said, Jason."

I rubbed my neck where the witch had squeezed me. "I was wrong about her having less power in the daytime," I said, slumping against the wall. I

42

felt defeated. "I don't know what we can do to stop her."

"We could nail the basement door closed," Lucy suggested.

But I knew that wouldn't work. "Ghosts get through locked doors," I said. "That won't stop them."

"Let's try it anyway," Lucy said. "It can't hurt."

Steve wasn't paying attention to us. He got to his feet and heaved a deep sigh of relief.

"Amazing," he said to himself. "I didn't wet my pants after all."

13

"What on earth are you kids doing?"

Startled, I whirled around and almost dropped the hammer on my toe. We'd been making so much noise nailing the basement door shut I hadn't heard the car or the front door.

"Mom! I didn't expect you so early. How is Katie?" I asked, dropping the rest of the nails in my pocket.

"Hello, Mrs. Winter," said Steve with a guilty look on his face.

"Hi, Mrs. Winter," said Lucy. "How was your trip?"

"Fine, Lucy, thank you," said Mom, looking distracted. She turned to me. "Jason, your dad and I need to talk to you. The doctors say Katie's head injury isn't serious but for some reason she's still not making sense — babbling about ghosts and witches. What exactly happened here last night?"

Lucy and Steve exchanged glances. "We'll be

going now," said Steve, edging toward the back door.

"But what is this?" said Mom, her glance catching on a half-hammered nail. "Jason, what are you up to? Why are you nailing the basement door?"

"It's the witch," Lucy blurted. "She's in the basement. She's real. We saw her. Didn't we? Tell her, Steve, we saw her. She would have got Jason if we hadn't all been roped together. It was the witch who attacked Katie."

Steve nodded, his eyes on the floor. "It's true, Mrs. Winter. This house is haunted." He looked up at her and finished in a rush, "You shouldn't stay here!"

My heart soared! Mom had to believe us now. She couldn't think we were *all* making it up!

Could she?

Mom had a strange, baffled expression on her face as she looked at each of us, one after the other. She didn't say anything. Her hair looked limp and there were dark circles under her eyes.

"We saw it, Mom," I burst out. "Really we did."

"You children better go now," she said to Lucy and Steve. "Jason's dad and I have some catching up to do."

After my friends left Mom gestured at me to sit down at the kitchen table. "Dad will be right down," she said. "He's checking on Sally."

It was kind of solemn waiting for Dad. Mom

poured us each some juice but she didn't say anything, just kept giving me these worried looks. I was relieved to hear Dad's step on the stairs.

"Sally was really out," he said, coming into the kitchen. "She never even opened her eyes."

Then he stopped, seeing the expression on Mom's face. "What's up?" he asked, cocking his head worriedly at me.

But Mom spoke first. "I came in and found Jason and his friends nailing the basement door shut," she said.

Dad's face fell. I noticed he had dark circles under his eyes, too. He sat down at the table. "Maybe you'd better start at the beginning," he said.

It was a long afternoon. I told them everything. No matter how crazy it sounded I went ahead and told about it.

My stomach was in knots. I could tell they didn't believe me. They were trying to look understanding but the strain of it kept breaking through.

I felt like I was beating my brains out on a wall of soft pillows.

Finally Dad stood up. "Well, there's one thing we can check," he said. "This witch of yours is still nailed in the basement, right? Let's go find her."

14

Dad got his big torch flashlight out of the car. He pried the nails out of the door and headed down without hesitation. I followed, feeling queasy.

It was different going down there with Dad. For one thing his big light cut through the gloom like a knife through butter. All the junk looked lifeless and ordinary.

And I knew the witch would never show herself to Dad. I could feel those eyes burning holes in our backs as we picked our way through the junk. I could almost hear her cackling silently.

Dad shone his light into every corner but we didn't see a thing. No ghosts. Not even a mouse.

"What about the attic, Dad," I said when we were back in the kitchen with the basement door closed and bolted. "You can see what she's capable of up there." I was pretty sure from things that happened before, that Bobby couldn't fix things the witch did on her own.

"Okay, son. Let's take a look."

He marched all the way upstairs to the attic. I followed — my stomach felt rotten and my knees were shaky, but I couldn't let him go up there alone.

"I don't believe it!" Dad said, stepping into the attic.

The walls were still smashed up and there was broken plaster everywhere. So I hadn't imagined *this* attack, that was for sure.

My dad looked stunned and baffled as he examined the wreckage.

"See, Dad?" I couldn't help being a little excited. "Now do you believe me? Now do you see how dangerous it is in this house?"

"I see that something very strange has been going on," he said slowly. "This is awful. This kind of destruction is very serious."

He thought I did it!

"But Dad — "

"Let's go downstairs, son. We'll talk about this later."

I shivered, feeling cold from the roots of my hair to my toes.

Nobody said much at supper.

I wasn't hungry — the hamburgers tasted like sawdust to me. My brain was numb and I didn't know what to say.

I escaped to my room as soon as I could.

After a while I heard Mom and Dad go into the

living room. They were talking in quiet, urgent voices and I knew they were talking about me.

I opened my door and snuck down the hallway to the stairs.

"I can't believe Jason would deliberately smash up the attic," said Mom. "He's not like that. And what about the baby-sitter? She thought she saw something, too."

"I can't believe Jason would do it, either," Dad admitted. "But what other explanation is there? You're not saying you believe all this nonsense about a haunted house?"

"No, of course not. All I'm saying, Dave, is that I think we should move to another place for the rest of the summer. Ghosts or no ghosts, something weird is going on in this house."

"I suppose you're right," said Dad. "We're out of our depth with this. I'll go see the real estate agent in the morning."

I wanted to jump up and down for joy.

My parents still didn't believe in the haunting. But they were going to get us out of here. By tomorrow, maybe.

Sally and I could survive anything for one more night.

Couldn't we?

15

No matter how much I tossed and turned I just couldn't get to sleep that night.

I tried sitting up and staring out at the windows, but the tall, shadowy trees made the yard look spookier than ever. So I got back in bed and pulled the covers over my head and tried to relax.

Not a chance. A million thoughts were racing through my mind. Thoughts about the ghosts and what they really wanted and why it had been my rotten luck to spend summer vacation in a haunted house.

I even tried counting sheep, but nothing worked.

Maybe if I fixed myself a glass of warm milk. That was supposed to make you sleepy, right?

But that would mean getting up and going downstairs to the kitchen, and that was the last thing I wanted to do. Because whenever I ventured outside my room at night in this house, something terrible happened.

I was thinking about that when I heard somebody tiptoe down the hall to Sally's room. Must be
Mom, checking to see that my little sister was okay.

I lay there waiting, expecting to hear Mom go
back to her own room. But there was nothing.

Nothing but a faint, creaky noise.

Something was wrong.

I got up and went out into the darkened hallway.

Sally's door was a few inches open, like always.

And light was coming from the door. Not the
little night lamp by her bed, but a strange, glowing light.

I pushed open the door.

"Sally?" I whispered.

The bedclothes were rumpled and bunched up.
But the lump underneath was too small to be
Sally. Wasn't it?

Maybe I was wrong.

I tiptoed to the bed and eased the blanket back.
Winky, the stuffed bunny, lay in the center of the
mattress where Sally should have been.

The room seemed to get darker as the bottom
dropped out of my stomach.

I heard a moaning noise and whipped around,
only to realize it was coming from me.

Then I noticed that Sally's closet door was open.
She liked it closed. Maybe something had frightened her — a dream maybe — and she was hiding
in there.

Without Winky? I knew that was a no-hoper even as I tiptoed to the closet. The door creaked as I eased it open the rest of the way and looked in.

It was black in there. Totally dark.

I leaned in. "Sally?" No answer.

It was a deep closet. I got down on my hands and knees and poked my head in, hoping to see Sally curled up in a corner.

I didn't see Sally. But what I did see hit me like a punch in the stomach. Sally's favorite nubby blanket was balled up and stuck into the back of the closet like a rag!

I pulled out the old blanket. Was it my imagination or was it still warm? Sally might have been here just a moment ago. But where had she gone? Down the hall, maybe, to my parents' bedroom.

Right. She got scared and went to Mom and Dad.

Pleased with my new idea, I was starting to back out of the closet when I saw something much worse than a discarded balled-up blanket.

A faint light was coming from the back of the closet. A sickening, greenish light. And shimmering in the light, stuck in a crack in the wall, were two long blond hairs.

Sally's hair.

As I reached out the greenish light grew brighter and the crack shot up the length of the wall!

I fell back on my heels. A doorknob was forming before my eyes right in the wall! It was an old metal doorknob — and I knew what I was supposed to do if I wanted to get Sally back.

Swallowing past the huge lump in my throat, I made myself reach up and touch the doorknob. It was icy cold. But it turned easily.

The door that I knew couldn't be there swung open without a sound. Cold air poured out on me, smelling of things shut up for years.

In the green glowing light I saw a steep, narrow staircase disappearing up into darkness. There was a strange smell. A stink that made my nose wrinkle.

Shivering in the cold, I groped my way into the open doorway. I had to go up. That was the only way to save Sally! But the cold seeped through my clothes and gripped my heart in an icy fist.

Suddenly I recognized the smell.

The phantom stairway reeked of fear.

16

I crouched to fit through the strange little door. The stairs were so narrow my elbows scraped the damp stone walls as I climbed.

I was shivering. Shivering so hard I was afraid I might fall.

How could Bobby ever have gotten Sally to go up these stairs? Poor Sally! Wherever she was, I knew she was terrified.

"I'm coming, Sally," I said through chattering teeth. I'd never been so cold. This nightmare cold seeped into my bones and curled up there without getting any warmer as I climbed the stairs. Dreading every step.

The horrible dim green light moved with me but I still couldn't see where I was going.

Then suddenly I was at the top of the stairs. I was standing in front of a heavy wooden door with big metal hinges. Like the door to a dungeon.

A thick iron bar lay across it, as if to keep some huge monster from escaping. I put my ear to the door but there was no sound from the other side.

Of course, Sally could be screaming her head off in there and I wouldn't be able to hear her through that door.

The stink of fear was worse up here. It got into my nose and worked its way into my brain until I wanted to turn tail and run down those stairs like a gibbering idiot.

If I did that, Sally would be stuck behind this door with whoever or whatever put her there. She'd be stuck here forever on the other side of the ghost world.

With a tremendous effort, I blew out my breath and took hold of the iron bar. It was as heavy as it looked. But finally I lifted it out of its holders. I propped the bar against my leg and twisted the big metal ring that served as a doorknob.

With a shriek of metal on stone, the door opened.

I stared in surprise. It was Bobby's attic room! The old-fashioned bedroom from a long time ago.

The greenish light vanished and a sad gray light took its place. I stepped inside, bringing the iron bar with me. But as I looked around, the big door swung soundlessly shut behind me. I heard the sharp snick! of the lock.

My stomach felt hollow. But my first worry was finding Sally. Then I'd work out how to get out of here.

The room had no windows, just Bobby's narrow

little bed, battered toy chest, and rocking chair. Nothing else. No one else.

The air had a heavy feel to it, like fear and unhappiness mixed together for a long time.

I'd been here before, of course, and nothing good ever happened in this room. But the bed and chair were empty. There was nowhere for Sally to hide. I stared around me like I'd been struck stupid.

I'd been so sure Sally would be here. Now what?

Why did Bobby's ghost want me up here?

A tiny, far-off cry made the little hairs on my neck stand on end.

It was a desolate, hopeless cry. The cry of a child who didn't expect anyone to come.

Slowly I turned around, holding my breath.

17

The closet!

I found myself staring at a low door cut in the sloping wall.

That's where the cry was coming from.

I rushed to the door and grabbed the small knob. Locked. Of course. What else did I expect? Nothing was easy in this miserable old house.

My mind flashed on the iron bar. I'd left it propped against the wall inside the massive door.

In two steps I had it in my hand and turned back to the closet door. "Stand back, Sally," I yelled. "I'm going to break it down."

"Jason!" came Sally's voice, scared and joyful at the same time. "Help!"

"I'm coming," I shouted, bashing a hole in the door. In minutes I had the thing in splinters and seconds later Sally jumped into my arms.

"Bobby was in there forever," she said, her voice thick with crying. "No one would come let

57

him out. But I knew you would come. I told Bobby you would come."

"Bobby locked you in the closet to see if I would come?" My heart felt like a chunk of ice.

"Not really," said Sally. "It was a — a 'speriment. But I was really scared."

I clutched her to me, thinking black thoughts. We had to get out of this house!

But first, we had to get out of this room.

I hoisted Sally against my shoulder and started for the door. But there was no big ring on the inside. No doorknob, either.

I didn't think it would be as easy to break down as the closet door. But, then, it wasn't really there, was it? It was just the door Bobby's imagination had made. This whole place was just a ghostly nightmare, right? So why did everything feel so solid, so real?

"Stand back, Sally," I said, putting her on the floor and grabbing up the iron bar. I ran at the door as hard as I could, the bar straight out in front of me.

I braced myself for impact and wasn't at all prepared for what happened. The heavy bar kept going right through the door. The door made a sucking noise as it swallowed in the bar and spit me out.

I staggered backward and fell.

Sally screamed.

There was a brown blob in her hair and it was

moving. I grabbed at it and the blob dissolved all over my fingers.

Desperately I wiped my hand on my shorts.

I looked around us. The walls were moving, melting and oozing toward us. It was a small room and getting smaller, fast!

The room was turning to slime.

Slime dripped in long, gooey strings to the floor. I felt something land on my head and saw a fat, brown slug plop onto Sally's cheek.

She batted at it and smeared herself with goo.

The walls inched closer.

We were going to be smothered in slime.

Sally pulled at my hand. "In the closet," she cried. "Back in the closet!"

Amazingly, that splintered doorway was the only thing that wasn't melting out of shape. And there was light coming from inside it.

Sally scrambled inside. It didn't look like there was room for me. I felt the room lap at my shoe.

No, I wasn't going to fit.

The wall made sucking noises as it ate my shoe.

Slime crept up my ankle.

18

"Come on, Jason," screamed Sally, yanking at my hair. "Come on!"

Shuddering with disgust and terror, I strained with all my might to free my foot.

But what was the use?

"Jason, there's a door," cried Sally. "Hurry!"

I jerked my head up.

Bright light blinded me. Behind it I thought I could make out stairs.

My heart pounded with hope. I yanked my foot out of the wall and scrambled into the closet. Squinting in the light I let Sally take my hand and lead me onto the stairs.

Behind us the closet door, whole once again, slammed shut.

What did Bobby have in store for us next?

The blinding light winked out, leaving millions of red spots in front of my eyes.

"Bobby saved us," said Sally cheerfully. As my

eyes adjusted I could see a smear on her cheek that looked like a squashed worm.

I sucked in my breath, realizing where we were.

We were on the attic stairs. The regular attic stairs. The *real* attic stairs. Above us the door was shut, although I could hear faint eating-type sounds behind it. Below us, the hall door was open and faint moonlight filtered up.

"I want to go downstairs," said Sally. "I want Winky."

"Winky's in your bedroom," I said, lifting her into my arms.

I went down the stairs, almost expecting they'd dissolve into goo under my feet. But the steps stayed rock solid and I was able to get Sally back to her bedroom without anything bad happening.

"There's Winky!" Sally murmured sleepily. "Just like you promised!"

I tucked her in and patted her on the head.

"You're the best brother in the world," Sally said.

And then she fell asleep.

Back in my own bedroom, I suddenly felt exhausted. Totally whipped. I was barely able to crawl into bed before I collapsed and closed my eyes. Another few seconds and I'd be out like a light.

Out like a light.

But it was the light that was keeping me awake. A blue glowing light coming from the walls.

I sat up.

Not again! I couldn't stand this! I *had* to get some sleep!

The blue light was coming from the mirror on the closet door. Once before Bobby had left messages on the mirror there. Now it was glowing again.

I rubbed my eyes and looked at the mirror.

The mists in the glass were darker this time, like thunderclouds. Clouds swirling thickly, boiling, and blowing apart as if something inside was fighting for control.

And when the mists cleared, I could see a coffin in the mirror. No, not a coffin, an old trunk. An old trunk like the trunk in the cellar.

As I watched in horror, the lid of the trunk opened. Something came out of the trunk, reaching up to the other side of the mirror.

A skeleton hand.

The fingertip of the skeleton hand glowed. Slowly the hand began to write on the other side of the mirror.

FIND THE WITCH

19

When I opened my eyes again it was morning. All night I'd been dreaming about the skeleton inside that old trunk, and the message Bobby left me on the mirror.

I didn't care what the little ghost wanted me to do — I wasn't going down in that basement again. No way! Even the thought was enough to almost make me barf.

I leaped out of bed and ran to the bathroom to brush my teeth. I shuddered as I looked in the bathroom mirror. Don't you dare leave me another message, I thought.

And then a feeling of relief flooded me.

I wouldn't have to FIND THE WITCH like the ghost wanted. Because today was the day Dad was going to see about getting us out of here!

That thought made me feel so cheerful I even felt hungry all of a sudden. I couldn't wait to get downstairs and get some of that breakfast I could smell cooking.

As I hurried toward the stairs I heard giggling coming from Sally's room. My heart flip-flopped. I couldn't help but feel a little bad about leaving Bobby in the lurch. I only hoped he didn't know that what we had planned.

I tiptoed down the hall to Sally's room.

"No, silly," I heard Sally say. "You can come home with me."

There was a short silence, then Sally said, "Yes, you can so come. I want you to come."

I poked my head around the door. Sally was sitting on the side of her bed holding Winky, her stuffed bunny, and talking to her invisible friend, Bobby.

"Hi, Sally," I said brightly. "You okay this morning?"

Sally turned and smiled at me. "Bobby is such a silly," she said, hopping down off the bed. "He thinks we're going to go away and leave him."

I brushed her hair back from her face, feeling uneasy. "Let's go have breakfast," I said.

Dad was sitting at the table when we went into the kitchen.

He ruffled Sally's hair and stood up, a stiff look on his face. "Jason, why don't you grab a muffin and walk outside with me while your mother gives Sally her breakfast."

Uh-oh. Trouble City. But I hadn't done anything!

As we walked out to the spot under the cherry

tree, I ticked off the possibilities in my head. Had the witch smashed up the garage? Or slashed Dad's tires?

But Dad didn't look like he was mad when he looked at me and cleared his throat. "I went down to the realtors this morning," he began.

Great!

"Your mother thought maybe we should move, considering what happened here while we were gone. Well, it turns out there isn't another place available for fifty miles around. It is the height of the summer, after all."

The corn muffin turned to lead in my stomach.

"But while I was at the realtors," Dad went on gravely, "I heard something that explains what happened here the other night."

My head shot up. Did he finally believe me? Could it really be?

"Seems there was another place vandalized just a couple blocks away. It was a vacant cottage and whoever it was really tore the place apart — kicked and stove in the walls, knocked holes in the roof, smashed up the little furniture that was there. A real mess." Dad shook his head.

I knew what was coming.

"I talked to the police chief and he thinks the same gang is responsible for what happened here. Our place has been empty for years and with it being dark and no car in the driveway they must have thought it was still vacant. Then you kids surprised them and Katie got hurt. I suppose we were lucky it wasn't worse."

I felt like a black cloud just opened over my head. And it was never going to go away. "But, Dad — "

"The chief doesn't think they'll be back. He figures you scared them almost as much as they scared you. But he'll be sending a cruiser by regularly, especially at night. I don't know that it's any better than ghosts, son, but I thought it might set your mind at rest."

I knew it was no use arguing. I pretended to be convinced by this story about the vandals and by the time Steve called for me, Mom and Dad were feeling more relaxed.

Steve and I decided to go mess around at the lake.

"We'll take Sally along with us, Mom," I said.

Mom smiled as if she was lucky to have a son like me. "That would be great, Jason," she said. "Your dad and I still have a lot of work to do on the Hartsville project."

My mom and dad are architects, designing a town complex for Hartsville. The sooner they were done, the sooner we could leave the house on Cherry Street and go back home.

While we walked down to the lake, I filled Steve in on what had happened with my parents while Sally ran on ahead with her plastic pail and shovel.

"We're never going to get out of that house," I

said dejectedly, kicking a stone into the smooth surface of the lake. "The ghosts are going to win."

"We'll think of something," said Steve. "Here comes Lucy. Maybe she'll have an idea."

He waved and Lucy came running down, black ponytail flying. She ran past us and leaped into the lake, splashing water in all directions. Steve and I were soaked.

A minute later we were all splashing each other and laughing and I almost forgot about my troubles.

We took turns keeping an eye on Sally. She couldn't really swim but she thought she could and she kept wanting to go out too deep and play with the big kids.

The lake was really warm that day and we didn't get out of the water until we were starved.

As we got dried off I knew there was only one thing to do. I described to Steve and Lucy the message Bobby had written in my mirror.

"The witch is down there," I said. "We found that out the hard way, and Bobby wants us to check out that old trunk, that's why he showed it to me in the mirror. The basement is where we'll find the secret to everything! That's why the old witch doesn't want us down there."

Steve and Lucy avoided my eyes.

"This time I'm going to get that trunk no matter what," I said. "Who wants to come with me?"

Lucy and Steve looked at each other, then at me.

"I gotta go," said Lucy, throwing her towel over her shoulder and scampering up the little beach. "See you guys later."

I turned to Steve.

He darted away from me. "Hey, Sally," he called. "Want a piggyback ride?"

Sighing deeply, I started after them.

I'd just have to do it myself.

20

"Find the witch. Find the witch," I repeated, trying to psych myself up.

I went upstairs for my flashlight and a baseball bat. This time I was on my own and I wanted the bat for protection.

I checked around and discovered that Sally was taking her nap and Mom and Dad were working in their office. So no one would interrupt me.

That was good, right?

I opened my bedroom door and immediately slipped on something. I slid right across the room. Whaaat?

Glancing down, I saw bits of myself looking up at me from all over the floor.

As I caught my balance my foot skidded again and I almost fell. My feet crunched. There were big chunks of mirrored glass all over the floor!

Then I looked across the room and didn't see myself.

The mirror in the closet door was gone! Smashed to pieces.

Obviously the witch had taken her sledgehammer to my mirror. And I knew why.

It was because of the message Bobby had put there last night.

That proved I was on the right track.

I swept up the broken glass, then headed back downstairs, keeping the image of the trunk in the front of my mind. I wouldn't think about anything else. I'd get it and get out.

The witch was scared, right? That's why she smashed my mirror. Maybe she was even more scared than me.

Don't think about being scared, Jay, I told myself. Don't think at all — just do it.

I unbolted the basement door. It creaked loudly as it swung open.

Get a grip, Jay. Grab that trunk and get out before the witch-thing knows you're there.

I took a deep breath, flipped on the light switch, and plunged down the stairs.

There, I'd made it. And nothing had touched me. But where was the trunk?

I stopped, my heart pounding, and looked around frantically.

The old trunk wasn't where it was supposed to be.

I gritted my teeth in a panic. The witch-thing

must have seen me by now. Any second she'd come roaring out of the shadows.

Then I saw it!

The trunk was pushed back against the wall, almost hidden behind a tall stack of boxes.

I waded into the mess, pushing boxes out of my way, heaving lamps and footstools and old shoes to the side to make a path.

Not only did I have to reach the trunk, the second part of my plan was to drag it back up with me.

I was making a lot of noise and concentrating on reaching my goal as fast as possible. So it was no surprise I didn't hear her behind me.

It was the stink that warned me.

21

All of a sudden I was gagging from the gar-bagey, dead-for-a-hundred-years smell.

I spun around.

The witch-thing leaped from behind a box, her eyes glowing in the dark.

"Arrrrrgggggg! You miserable boy!" shrieked the creature.

Her sharp claws sank through the material of my shirt.

Riiiip!

My shirt tore as I slung her off me in terror.

She hissed, yellow eyes glowing and quick as a flash I raised the baseball bat and swung. I heard a crunch as the bat connected.

"Ahheeee!" The witch screamed and vanished back into the shadows.

I was breathing hard but there was no time to rest. I grabbed the handle of the trunk.

It was lighter than I expected.

But what had I thought was in it? A body?

I heaved and hauled the trunk through the path I'd sort of made, banging into boxes and knocking things over.

Then I was clear of the mess of junk and halfway to the stairs. The bottom of the trunk scraped over the dirt floor as I dragged it, my breath sounding ragged in my ears.

I reached the stairs and started humping it up, making an awful racket.

My heart was ready to burst with effort.

Suddenly a black shape darted out of the darkness and rushed me.

The witch was back. Hissing and spitting, she grabbed hold of the handle on the other end of the trunk.

"Mine!" she moaned. *"Mine!"*

I yanked back harder but I was nearly out of strength.

She pulled the trunk down a step, then another, dragging me down, too.

The witch had won again — but I couldn't let go.

My hand seemed permanently frozen to that handle. She was pulling my arm right out of its socket!

Gritting my teeth against the pain, I started to imagine all the horrible things the creature would do to me when she got me back down into the basement.

"The trunk is mine!" she hissed. *"And so are you!"*

Panic rushed through my veins.

With the last of my strength I braced my feet on the stairs, gripped the handle as hard as I could, and tugged with all my might.

The other handle broke!

The witch-thing tumbled down the stairs with an awful screech and sprawled on the dirt floor.

"*I'll get you!*" the creature moaned. "*I'll get you yet!*"

Then she scuttled back into the shadows like a wounded thing.

Losing no time, I hauled the trunk up into the kitchen.

Safe at last! Totally out of breath, I collapsed against the basement door — after bolting it shut.

A door opened down the hall.

"Jason? Is that you?"

"Yes, Mom." I jumped guiltily. Where could I hide the trunk?

"What was all that noise? Is everything okay?"

"Noise?" I moved into the hallway so she wouldn't have to come into the kitchen to talk to me.

Mom had a blue pencil behind her ear and a calculator in her hand. "Clattering, banging. Was that you?"

Dad's voice came from inside the room. "Carol, I need you to look over these calculations. We may have a problem here."

"I was just playing, Mom," I assured her, disappointed she hadn't heard the witch's screeching.

She gave me one of those considering looks, the kind that meant she was suspicious about my answer.

My heart sank. In a minute she'd come into the kitchen and see the trunk and demand all kinds of explanations. Then my dad called her again and she reached a decision.

She turned back into the office.

"We're going to be working a while longer," said Mom. "Maybe you could look in on Sally."

"Sure, Mom."

I went back to the kitchen. I couldn't leave the trunk here. I'd have to carry it up to my room. Mom almost never went in there. She might not even see it.

I called up Steve and got him to come over. He was eager to help now that it was out of the basement. We hauled it up to my room and set it in the center of the floor.

"What do you think is in there?" asked Steve, his eyes bright.

"The truth," I said. "The solution to the haunting."

22

I knelt in front of the trunk.

I was excited but scared, too. Who knew what was really inside, or why the ghosts were fighting over it?

"You'd better stand by the door, Steve," I said. "You can run for help if we need it."

The leather of the trunk was cracked and dry. My fingers trembled as I reached for the clasp.

Well, I thought, here goes. With still-shaking fingers I undid the clasp.

As I swung it open, the lid made a tremendous skreeky noise, like bones being pulled apart.

"What's in it?" cried Steve breathlessly.

I stared in disappointment. The witch-thing must have gotten everything already. "Nothing," I sighed. "Just a few scraps of paper."

I lifted out torn pieces of newspaper. They were crumpled, like they might have been used to wrap something. But what?

"What's that ribbon?" asked Steve, pointing over my shoulder.

"Ribbon?" There, caught in a corner of the trunk was a red ribbon. I pried at it, starting to feel excited.

A ribbon just like it had been tied around the letters I'd seen when Steve and I first found this trunk, weeks ago, but those old letters had disappeared before I ever got a chance to read them.

Slowly the ribbon came free — and with it some flattened papers! I slid the ribbon off. Here was the answer, I just knew it!

There were only two letters in the little bundle. I unfolded the first one and read:

Dear Alice,

I am beside myself with worry over the ruby. I can't imagine where it could be. Did you look in the case in my room? I thought I packed it but it's possible I never did.

We are retracing our steps in a desperate hope of finding the jewel. It's the only inheritance I have from my mother and without it all our hopes for the next few years are dashed.

If you find it please telegraph me at once.

Take good care of little Bobby and give him a big kiss from his mom and dad.

Affectionately,
Sarah Wood

A missing jewel? The witch-thing had been screaming something about a jewel that night in the attic. But what would a ruby have to do with Bobby?

I spread out the second letter, hoping it would have some answers.

> *Dear Alice,*
> *We've nearly given up hope of ever recovering the jewel. I'm afraid we're going to be too poor to keep you on as a nanny for the next few years. But don't worry. We'll give you an excellent reference.*
>
> *Our last hope is that the ruby is still somewhere in the house. We're making plans to be home by next week and I'll turn the place upside down looking for it. I can't believe it's really gone!*
>
> *Tell Bobby how much we love him and miss him.*
>
> > *Affectionately,*
> > *Sarah Wood*

I looked at the date on the top of the letter. It was written just a week before Bobby died. But I didn't see how any of this solved the mystery.

Then it started to make sense, sort of. The jewel the witch-thing was looking for must be this same ruby Bobby's mother had lost!

I turned to tell Steve. He was smoothing out a sheet of crumpled newspaper.

"There's stuff in here about Bobby," he said, sounding excited. "All about how he died and everything."

I scooted over and grabbed the paper, feeling my heart quicken once again. But there wasn't anything I didn't already know from the papers Katie and I had found in the attic.

The newspaper described the tragic death of little Bobby Wood. He'd fallen from the cherry tree in his backyard while his parents were in Europe. Only the nanny, Alice Everett, had been home at the time of the accident.

"But Jason," said Steve, frowning, "how could Bobby fall from the cherry tree? When you hear him at night, doesn't he fall from the top of the stairs?"

"Exactly," I said. "The newspapers got it wrong, that's one thing I'm sure of."

"Hey, here's more," said Steve excitedly. "Something about a missing teddy bear and a big ruby."

"What?" I snatched it from him.

"Hey! I found it first," Steve complained.

"Yeah, but it's my ghost," I reminded him.

The beginning of the article told of Bobby's death again. Then it said: *In an odd coincidence, the child's favorite plaything, an old teddy bear, is nowhere to be found and the same is true of the Wood family's most prized possession, a magnificent ruby. The jewel was left to Mrs. Wood by her mother and provided the collateral for her husband's business loan. If the ruby is not recovered it is expected Mr. Wood will lose his business. And if the teddy bear is not found, a little boy will go to his grave alone."*

"That's creepy," said Steve. "What's 'collateral' mean?"

Proud to know a word Steve didn't, I dug into what I could remember of my parents' conversations. "It means something valuable. You take the jewel to a bank and ask the bank to lend you some money. Then if you can't pay them back the money they keep the collateral — the jewel, in this case. But since the ruby was missing, the bank must have taken Mr. Wood's business instead."

Steve looked disappointed. "Oh. Well, I don't see what all that has to do with ghosts," he said, tossing the bits of paper back into the trunk.

"No," I said slowly. "I don't, either."

But I knew there was a connection. Bobby's ghost wanted me to figure it out, that's why he'd urged me to look in the trunk.

And that worried me. Bobby was just a little kid. He expected older people to understand what he meant. When they didn't he was likely to have a tantrum.

And Bobby's ghostly tantrums were the most terrifying things I'd ever seen.

23

That night I asked for a glass of warm milk before I went to bed, just as a precaution.

"I hope you're not staying up too late, reading those scary books of yours," Mom said as she handed me the milk.

"Not a chance," I said. "Tonight I'm going straight to sleep."

"Good," Mom said with a smile. "That's exactly what you need. You've been exhausted lately, overdoing it. And you know what happens when you overdo it."

"Right," I said. "My imagination gets out of control."

She was wrong about my imagination getting out of control, but I'd given up trying to convince her the house was haunted. The ghosts didn't show themselves to adults, so adults thought they didn't exist.

A pretty neat trick, if you happened to be a ghost.

The warm milk trick seemed to work. As soon as my head hit the pillow I started to doze off. Dreaming about baseball, and swimming, and how I couldn't wait to get back to our own house . . .

I woke up with a jolt, every nerve tingling. I gripped the sides of the bed, my eyes wide.

There was some kind of vibration in the air.

BONNNG!

The grandfather clock! It must have already chimed at least once and woke me up. I lay rigid, waiting for it to strike again.

The broken grandfather clock in the hall only chimed when a haunting was about to happen.

Dread sat on my chest, making it hard to breathe. I hated the waiting. I hated lying helpless, straining my ears for the first sound of a little kid's scared footsteps. I knew what was coming — and I knew there was nothing I could do to stop it.

The haunting had started.

Outside my bedroom door Bobby's ghost was crying. Then I heard his small feet hitting the floor as he ran.

He was running in fear. Crying so hard he was hiccuping.

Running and running, the thud of heavier footsteps chasing him, getting louder and louder as the sound of his crying went higher and higher.

Then I heard the witch's voice screaming at him.

"Come back here, you little brat! Give me that jewel!"

The little boy kept running. His feet went right by my door. Followed a heartbeat later by the thudding of the witch-thing, screaming, *"It's mine! Mine!"*

I tensed up, waiting. Because I knew what was going to happen. It was always the same, whenever the haunting started.

The little boy kept running. The witch-thing kept chasing him.

And then —

CRUNCH!

The little boy smashed through the railing at the end of the hallway and fell to the floor below.

"Heellllllllllllpppp meeeeeeeeee!"

His awful, falling scream cut through me like a knife.

If I lived here fifty years — which I wouldn't — I would never get used to that terrible sound.

The house fell silent. Sometimes that was the end of the haunting and after a while I could turn over and go back to sleep.

But sometimes it was just the beginning of something even more terrifying.

I lay with my hands at my sides staring straight up into the darkness, Bobby's dying cry banging around inside my head.

No way had Bobby died in a fall from the cherry tree, like it said in the paper. He died the way I heard him die night after night. Hurtling over the stairway while someone chased him!

It had to be the nanny, Alice Everett. Bobby's nanny was the witch-thing, the old lady who'd stayed on in the empty house until she died. The old witch whose body had never been found.

She was the one who had moved Bobby's body from the house to under the cherry tree, so no one would know it was her fault that he'd died.

Boys fall out of trees, right? Accidents happen. Everybody believed her at the time.

But why had she been chasing the little boy? Was it Bobby who had stolen the jewel from his mother? Was the old witch-thing still trying to get it back, even when she was a ghost haunting the same house as Bobby?

Suddenly a sound outside the room blotted out my thoughts.

Something was scratching at my door.

I held my breath and concentrated on seeing in the dark. Fear was all around me — a cold tingling all over my body.

The knob was turning! The door began to open.

Maybe it's my mom, checking up on me, I thought hopefully.

A foul smell invaded the room.

Not Mom.

I dove out of bed and rolled underneath.

24

I peeked out and couldn't see a thing. But I could hear it. Something had come into my room. I could hear it wheezing.

Under the bed probably wasn't the best place to hide. Too obvious. But too late now — I couldn't move without giving myself away.

Heavy breathing. The rustle of old clothing. The invisible thing was coming closer.

Peering into the darkness, I tried to follow the sounds. Who was it and what did they want with me?

Then I got another whiff of that foul stench. Only the witch-thing smelled like that.

The ghost of a child killer was in the room with me!

I peeked out from under the bed and saw the bottom part of her black cloak trailing along the floor. That was the rustling noise.

The cloak moved back and forth across the room.

Suddenly I knew what it wanted. The trunk. The dead creature had come to take back the trunk!

The old trunk was stored in my closet. But the papers and letters I'd found inside it were someplace even safer.

Under my pillow.

What a goon! What had I been thinking — that was the most obvious place. And if the foul creature found the letters, she'd find me hiding under the bed!

I had to do something, and fast.

The door to my closet creaked open.

The witch cackled with satisfaction as she fumbled with the trunk latch. The lid creaked open.

This was it! The only chance I'd have.

I slid out from under the bed and snaked my hand up over the side, feeling for my pillow. My hand found the letters. I snatched them and quickly ducked back under the bed.

"Nooooo!"

The witch hissed with fury. Had she seen me?

Her black cloak crackled. Her breath rattled, filling the room with its putrid stink. Her sticklike arm shot out angrily, sweeping across the top of my bureau. Books and airplane models clattered to the floor.

"I'll get you, you little brat," she croaked.

I scrambled farther under the bed until my back

was against the wall and clutched the papers to my chest.

Footsteps approached the bed.

I tried to shrink myself smaller.

Suddenly the bed was lifted off the floor as the creature let out another angry bellow. She flung the mattress against the wall and it slid back down. I was still hidden.

The dead thing grunted as she bent to look under the bed. I held my breath, trying not to shake so hard.

I knew she had me.

I flattened myself against the wall.

Screeee . . . screeeee . . .

Her claws scraped the floor an inch from my face.

25

Scrunching my eyes shut, I waited for her claw to shoot out and snag me. I tried to think of a way to get out of this but my brain was in slow motion.

I'll kick and scream, I thought. Maybe Mom and Dad would hear me.

Her garbagey breath was suffocating. My skin crawled as I waited for her to grab me.

But nothing happened.

Then I heard soft, evil laughter, moving away. As if the witch had thought of something worse than grabbing me.

My bedroom door closed softly.

She was gone.

I counted to a hundred to be sure and then crawled out from under the bed, a queasy feeling stirring in my stomach.

I should have been relieved. I had won, hadn't I? At least for now.

But the old witch-thing was up to something.

Her laughter echoed in my brain, sending fear rippling up and down my spine.

I put the letters in an old paper bag and stuck them under the trunk in the closet. She'd already looked in the trunk. She'd never look there again.

As I started to close the closet door, the empty mirror frame started to glow with a blue light. The mirror reappeared on the door and the mist began to swirl.

Blood rushed to my head.

I bolted for the door. The knob turned uselessly in my hand, round and round. I couldn't get the door open!

"Bobby!" I shouted angrily, "Open this door! The witch is going after Sally. You have to let me out right this second."

The image of the little boy swam in the mist. He looked sad.

I tried the door again but it still wouldn't open. Anger swelled in my chest like a giant bubble.

I grabbed the first thing that came to hand — my Boy Scout hatchet — and heaved it at the mirror as hard as I could.

But the satisfying sound of shattering glass didn't come. Instead the hatchet blade sank into the mirror and vanished with a faint pop!

From the mirror the ghostly image of Bobby just looked at me with a sad expression. He was glowing, filled with the blue light.

As I watched in horrified amazement he raised

a finger and began to write another message on the other side of the mirror. This time the message was different.

I scowled, reading, "THE SECRET IS IN THE ATTIC."

My anger started charging up again. "Whatever happened to 'Find the witch'? That was the message last night, right? So I got the trunk, I found the witch," I shouted. "What about that?"

But the image began to fade, taking the light with it.

What was going on here?

26

I was alone in the dark bedroom.

All around me the house was deathly quiet.

Had the witch already grabbed Sally while Bobby kept me in here trying to get me to do stuff by making up spooky messages?

Sally was so trusting. She would never suspect anyone wanted to harm her. It would be easy to get her to go along with anything.

One thing for sure. I was *not* going to the attic.

I had to get to Sally.

I rushed at the door. If it still wouldn't open, I'd smash it down.

But as I grabbed for the knob, the door swung open on its own. It caught me on the shoulder and knocked me back inside the room, flat to the floor.

The hall outside the door was pitch-dark, like the rest of the house. Dark and deathly quiet.

I pushed myself up cautiously. What now? There was no sign of the dead witch-thing.

Then I heard it.

Out in the hall. Small squeaky sounds, coming closer.

It sounded like Sally, pulling a toy. Only there were no footsteps. Just the *squeee-uup, squeee-uup* of small wheels.

"Go back to bed, Sally," I called out. Hoping it was my little sister.

There was no answer.

The house seemed to snatch up the sound of my voice and bounce it from wall to wall. It felt like the house was laughing at me.

The squeak of the little wheels got louder as whatever-it-was rolled along the hallway coming closer, heading for me.

I scrambled to my feet. Maybe it would go on past my room. All I wanted was to get to Sally's room, make sure my little sister was all right.

The trundling noise stopped. It was right outside my door. My heart sank.

My eyes popped as a small red wagon turned and glided through the open door into my room.

The wagon was empty. And no one was pulling it.

All of a sudden, my muscles turned to soup and all the strength went out of my body. I flopped onto the floor like one of Sally's rag dolls. I couldn't move.

The little red wagon rolled toward me and bumped gently against my knees. All I could do was stare at it helplessly.

Suddenly I felt invisible fingers grip my shoulders and reach under my knees. The ghostly hands were gentle but I shuddered at their cold touch. I hated not being able to at least fight back.

The invisible hands lifted me up and laid me down in the wagon.

The wagon began to move.

27

The wagon rolled on its squeaky wheels out of my room and down the hall.

I was frozen in place. I couldn't even turn my head to see if anyone — Sally? the witch-thing? — was following. But I heard no footsteps.

"If you'll just let me up," I whispered through clenched teeth, "I'll come where you want. I promise."

But the ghosts weren't listening.

Between feeling silly and angry and scared out of my wits, I couldn't think what to do. I was as helpless as a baby.

As the wagon approached, the door to the attic stairs opened, spilling darkness over me. The stairway was inky black. The hairs on the back of my paralyzed neck prickled.

Something was waiting for us up there. Something so terrible I couldn't even think about it.

Mentally I braced myself for a bumpy ride, but the wagon floated up the stairway.

A faint yellow light beckoned from above.

My heart felt like it was being squeezed between powerful hands. I wanted to scream but my throat stayed closed.

The red wagon glided to a stop at the top of the stairs.

This wasn't the smashed-up attic I'd left this morning. It was a tiny windowless room with a small bed and a battered toy box and a rocking chair. Bobby's old room.

There was light, but it was a cold light. Light from long ago.

Creeeak-creak.

The rocking chair. There was someone in it.

Suddenly I could move. Blood flowed into my muscles and I jumped out of the wagon.

The rocking chair slowly swiveled toward me. Would it be Sally? Brought here as a warning? Or Bobby himself? Or — I shuddered — the witch?

I gasped in shock. It wasn't any of them.

It was nothing. Just a stuffed teddy bear. And an old ratty one at that.

What was this all about? Was the ghost scaring me just for the fun of it?

The chair began to rock again. And as it rocked it moved across the floor toward me. The mangy teddy bear was staring at me with its beady little eyes.

Eyes that looked almost alive.

Time to get out of here. The thing gave me the

serious creeps! I backed away. Feeling behind me for the doorway.

The attic door slammed shut, barely missing my fingers.

I whirled around and began tugging on the doorknob, though I already knew it was hopeless, trying to fight the house.

My shoulder blades tensed an instant before I heard the voice behind me, as if something in me expected it.

"I am the secret."

It was a gruff, lispy voice, like a little kid trying to make his voice go deep.

Slowly I turned around.

The teddy bear was talking to me. And its button eyes were glowing.

"I am the secret," it said again, as if trying to convince me. *"Please save me."*

I almost felt sorry for it, it was so mangy-looking and pathetic. It reminded me a little of Sally's stuffed bunny, Winky.

Except Winky never talked or made doors shut in your face.

"Let me out of here," I demanded forcefully.

The bear slipped down until it was lying on the seat. It slid across the seat on its back and flopped over the edge. It waggled its feet and jumped to the floor. I stared in horrified fascination.

One raggedy, mended ear fell forward over an

eye as it looked at me. *"You can help,"* it said. Its mouth didn't move.

It took a shaky step toward me and fell over onto its face. *"Save me,"* it said into the floor.

As the bear struggled upright, I scooted along the wall and crouched in a corner, pulling the rocking chair around like a barrier in front of me.

The teddy bear hesitated, then got itself turned in my direction. Reaching out its arms, it marched toward me like a miniature zombie. *"Save me. Please save me."*

Its soft, furry paw touched me.

I shuddered as the teddy bear climbed onto my knee. Then instead of climbing higher, it slipped away.

Surprised, I opened my eyes.

The teddy bear was heading for the toy box. The lid opened and the worn-out old bear climbed up inside, pulling the lid down after it.

But what about the secret? What was I supposed to do now?

I heard the click of a lock.

The attic door swung open and light streamed into the little room from the stairway. It was morning already!

Forget about the teddy bear and its stupid secret — all I wanted to do was get out of there. I was almost out the door when a small creaking noise stopped me.

I looked over my shoulder. The lid of the toy box stood open.

The smart thing would be to keep going, down the stairs.

Instead I walked over and looked into the toy box. Empty. I swallowed a pang of surprise and disappointment. I hadn't learned anything new. How could I save me and Sally — and Bobby — if I couldn't figure out the mystery?

Had all this been to get me out of the way? To keep me away from Sally?

But as I dashed for the door the toy box lid slammed down twice. Like it was trying to get my attention. Reluctantly, I went back and peered inside.

There *was* something there!

28

More newspaper.

I was excited but disappointed too. All the newspaper stories I'd found had been confusing, full of things I knew couldn't be true.

The old newspapers had told me who Bobby was and when he died but they all said he died falling from the cherry tree and I knew that couldn't be true. I'd heard Bobby falling from the top of the stairs, many times.

Well, I didn't want to read anything up here. Sticking the yellowed paper under my arm, I hurried down the attic stairs.

Morning sunlight streamed through the hallway. From downstairs came the sounds and smells of breakfast. I heard Sally giggling as Mom playfully teased her.

Suddenly I was hungry enough to eat a horse. Something about fighting ghosts gave me a huge appetite.

But before I could go down to breakfast I had

to put the old newspapers away. I hurried into my bedroom, started to whip open the closet door — and stared in disbelief.

The hatchet.

It was buried deep in the closet door. Right in the spot where I'd thrown it through the haunted mirror.

Good thing Mom hadn't been in here to see that!

I sat down on my bed to calm my racing heart and figured I might as well look through the bits of newspaper from the toy box.

Good thing I did. Because in the old papers was a clue. And the clue gave me an idea that changed everything.

"Jason, slow down, you'll make yourself sick."

I looked up from my second plate of strawberry waffles. "I'm just hungry."

"Fine," said Mom. "But what's the hurry?"

I opened my mouth to tell her, and then thought better of it. She'd heard enough ghost stuff.

After breakfast I called up Steve and Lucy.

"Get your butts over here," I whispered into the phone. "I think I've solved the haunting."

My two buds hurried right over. Steve was grinning from ear to ear as he bounced up the porch steps. But Lucy looked more serious. "What happened?" she asked. "What did you find out?"

"Follow me," I said, leading them upstairs to my bedroom.

Once we were inside I shut the door and showed them the latest batch of old newspapers.

"Listen to this," I said, and read from the article that had caught my attention.

The search for the Wood family's missing ruby veered in a new direction yesterday as police questioned the bewildered nanny, Alice Everett, about its disappearance. A thorough search was made of the house. However, no progress was made, police admitted last night.

Miss Everett was too distraught to make any comment. The grief-stricken young woman was the only one present when the Woods' only child, Robert, was killed in a fall from a cherry tree.

Mrs. Wood, mother of the dead boy, said she was very upset that the nanny was a suspect in the matter of the missing ruby.

Mr. and Mrs. Wood are leaving the home where so many happy memories have become painful. Mrs. Wood said Miss Everett would be staying on as caretaker of the house.

"Wow!" said Lucy, wide-eyed. "The witch is the nanny!"

I nodded. "That's what I suspected, but this proves it. But why would the nanny kill Bobby?"

"Maybe Bobby knew what happened to the ruby and she didn't want him to tell," Steve suggested.

Lucy clapped her hands together. "Yes!" she

exclaimed. "It's finally starting to make sense."

"Could be," I said. "The witch-thing is the ghost of the nanny, Alice Everett. She lived in this house for years after Bobby died. And when she died, she became a ghost, too."

Steve shook his head in disbelief. "I wonder if the old lady knew Bobby was haunting the house before she died."

"Maybe Bobby hid the ruby," said Lucy excitedly. "That's why the old lady was so mean and never went anywhere."

"Or she just hid the ruby herself out of meanness," said Steve.

I nodded at them solemnly. "I think the ruby is still in the house," I said. "And you guys are going to help me find it!"

29

"You know where we have to look first, don't you?" said Lucy, chewing anxiously on the end of her ponytail.

"Not the cellar!" Steve protested.

I nodded — Lucy was right. "That's where the witch hangs out," I said. "There must be a good reason."

"The nanny-ghost-witch doesn't want us to find the ruby," said Lucy. "That's why it's so scary down there."

Steve picked up my baseball bat and hefted it. "This time will be different," he vowed. "If that old beast comes after me, I'll swing for the bleachers. Pow!"

He took a cut with the bat that made the air whistle.

"Okay," he said. "Let's do it."

Mom had sent Sally off to some play group so we only had to lie low until my parents had shut themselves in their office.

"Everybody be as quiet as possible," I whispered as we gathered in the kitchen.

We roped ourselves together like mountain climbers, just like the last time we made an expedition into the cellar.

"It may look silly," said Lucy, double-knotting the rope at her waist, "but it sure worked."

Lucy and Steve both had baseball bats as weapons. A sudden inspiration made me take the fire extinguisher from the kitchen wall.

"Here goes nothing," I whispered, opening the basement door.

We all clicked on our flashlights and the beams sprang into the darkness.

I started down, the extinguisher held out in front of me like a machine gun. Let the old witch come for me! I'd blast her into smithereens.

The basement was as silent as a tomb.

"We'll have to look in every box, every toe of every shoe," I said, dumping a boxful of old boots onto the floor. "If that stolen ruby is here, we'll find it."

"That's right," said Lucy, a little more loudly than necessary. "And we'll just stay right here until we *do* find it."

"What if it's not here?" Steve said, alarmed, but Lucy and I didn't answer.

Lucy was sure we'd find the ruby. And I was sure the witch-nanny couldn't bear for us to be messing in her things.

We searched in silence for a few minutes, our ears tensed for any sound.

"Hey, Jason, get a load of this," teased Steve, pulling a battered straw hat from a box. "Just your size. You'll have to wear it on our next expedition."

I looked up and a movement behind Steve caught my eye.

But before I could get a better look there was a flash of light, a loud POP! and the sharp tinkle of shattering glass.

We were plunged into blackness.

30

"The lightbulb exploded," said Lucy in a tense whisper. She blended into the shadows.

The image of Steve's grin stayed behind my eyes like a photographic negative.

In a panic we shone our flashlights in every direction.

Cackling laughter sprang up and taunted us from every direction. Surrounded by the awful noise we huddled together, afraid to move.

HEEEEE-HEEEE-HEEEEEEEEEEEEEE!

"Get out!" screamed the witch-ghost. *"Get out or die!"*

"There!" screamed Steve.

Lucy and I pointed our flashlights. I caught a flash of black material slipping into the darkness, then lost it.

Our light beams were shaking. My knees, too. I was ready to give up. I swept my flashlight around, looking for the stairs.

Then something soft hit my face! I couldn't see! I was blinded.

The smell of death was filling my head and choking off my air.

My breath stopped. Dead air flowed down my throat and froze my lungs.

"Ahhhh!" screamed Steve. "She got me!"

I shook my head wildly but the clingy stuff stuck to my face.

Then something grabbed my shoulder. In a panic I flailed my arms and jerked away.

There were grunts of pain and rustling noises everywhere.

"Jason! Stop!" shouted Lucy. "Stay still."

I felt the soft, moldy stuff sliding across my face and then Lucy pulled it free. I gulped in air.

"It's throwing things at us," cried Lucy, holding up the dusty black scarf she'd pulled off my face.

"She hit me with a shoe," shouted Steve. He was swinging away with his bat but not hitting anything. "The heel got me right in the eye!"

"Wait, Steve," I said, grabbing his arm.

His chest heaved.

Anger raged in me like a fire. "Save your strength," I said through clenched teeth. "We're going to get her."

I hefted the fire extinguisher. "You two sweep the walls. And when you catch her in the light, keep her there!"

Lucy and Steve nodded grimly.

We advanced along the walls and shone our lights into every corner.

"Come and get us, witch!" taunted Steve.

"We know you killed poor little Bobby!" Lucy added.

"We're not afraid of you!" I joined in.

But the witch-thing stayed out of sight.

"Maybe if we go back to work," I whispered. "Like we're not afraid of anything."

"Yeah," said Steve, heaving a deep shaky breath. "That'll bring her out."

We opened some more boxes. Lucy kept biting her lip and looking over her shoulder.

I knew exactly how she felt. I was strung so tight I felt like another loud noise would snap me in two.

Something squealed in pain. *"EEEeee — "*

The cry was cut off suddenly. We heard the sound of small bones crunching. Then low laughter came out of the dark.

"That was a rat," spoke the witch in a voice that echoed off the ceiling and floor. *"Next time it will be you."*

Steve swung his light up while Lucy and I stood frozen in shock.

We knew the creature wasn't kidding. It wanted to squash us like rats.

"There," yelled Steve. "There she is!"

31

"**O**ver there!" cried Steve. "She disappeared behind those boxes!"

Steve lunged after the witch, dragging Lucy and me with him. He started prodding boxes with his bat, a frown of furious concentration on his face.

I kept my flashlight aimed over his shoulder, searching the darkness.

"Maybe this isn't such a good idea," said Lucy, hanging back.

"I know she's there," said Steve. "Unless she got on her broomstick and flew away, she's back there somewhere."

"Yes, but — " began Lucy.

She didn't get a chance to finish because a large box came shooting off the top of a tall stack, aimed right for Steve's head.

I gave him a shove but not quick enough. The box hit him and Steve went down with a painful OOOMF!

The witch cackled with triumph.

Something about that laughter made my blood boil. I saw her black form melt into the shadows and suddenly I couldn't stand to let her get away.

I fumbled at the knotted rope around my waist. I had to get free so I could go after her.

"Jason, don't!" cried Lucy, helping Steve up. "She'll get you. We have to stay together!"

I didn't answer. The knot slipped free and the rope dropped to the floor. I aimed my flashlight into the shadows and moved slowly toward the spot where I had last seen her.

There! A black form detached from the wall and darted sideways.

"No, you don't!" I shouted, and brought up the nozzle of the fire extinguisher. I pressed the trigger and foam jetted out.

Yes! Right on target!

"AAAAAEEEEEEEEEE!"

The witch writhed and howled and seemed to shrivel under the black cape.

I dropped the fire extinguisher and, without thinking, I leaped right on her.

I expected her bones to dissolve under my fingers, the ghost to slip away and leave me holding air. But my hands gripped bony shoulders. Real shoulders. Solid bones.

I was so surprised I almost jerked away. But I held on tight.

Slowly her head turned toward me. She hissed

through her broken teeth like a snake. "SSSSSSSSSSSSSSSSSSSSSSSSSSS."

Her awful smell filled my nostrils.

"Unhand me, brat, or I'll turn your innards to soup and eat them myself," she rasped from inside the black cape, sending stink waves over me with every word.

She writhed and squirmed. I clenched my teeth and held on.

Black spots began to appear before my eyes. The putrid fumes of her breath were getting to me. I was growing weaker.

I tried to call out to Steve and Lucy but the words gurgled in my throat.

The witch chuckled softly in my ear. *"Now I've got you, boy,"* she hissed.

I felt one of her sharp claws pierce my side.

32

Upstairs, the basement door opened.

"What's going on down there?" a voice demanded.

It was my dad.

The witch snarled. The pain in my side was so sharp one of my hands let loose.

"Jason's captured the witch, Mr. Winter!" Steve cried excitedly.

The witch jerked away but I held on. She was dragging me slowly into the shadows.

We heard my dad coming cautiously down the dark stairway. I wanted to scream at him to hurry, but the words stuck in my throat. I felt my heels dragging along the dirt floor as she struggled to escape.

Dad hesitated, squinting when Steve's flashlight beam caught him in the face.

"I can't see," he protested.

As Steve lowered the beam, the witch blasted me with her breath and slipped out of my grasp.

"Stop her!" Lucy shouted.

I grabbed the witch's cape but the oily material slipped through my hands.

I couldn't let her get away now! I couldn't! Where was Dad?

I launched myself into the air. My arms closed around the foul thing in an awful bear hug as we crashed to the floor.

The witch screamed with fury but this time I held on.

Suddenly a bright light fell over us. My dad had screwed in a new bulb, flooding the cellar with light.

Dad gasped. "Who is this?" he asked in a horrified voice.

"It's the ghost of the nanny," Lucy explained. "She's an evil witch."

Dad grasped her arm and helped the old witch gently to her feet. Carefully he lifted the hood of the cape. Light spilled onto the witch's ancient, wrinkled face. Her beady eyes blazed with spite and evil. She flinched away from the brightness, spitting and moaning.

"This is no ghost," Dad said sternly. "This woman is as flesh and blood as you or me." He turned to the witch. "Who are you? What are you doing in our basement?"

Baring her stumps of teeth, she snarled and shook off my hand. Squaring her shoulders, she rose in height and became the black-shrouded creature that roamed our house at night, destroying anything — and anyone — who got in her way.

"I'm Alice Everett," she said in a growly voice that sent shivers down my spine. "This is my house! Your smarty-pants son is trying to steal my ruby like the other one did. Trouble-making boys, it's all they're good for! But I'll fix them, like I fixed Bobby!"

She threw back her head and cackled wildly. "I'll take care of them kids!"

Then, quick as a cat, her arm came up in a blur and her claws raked my father's face. Dad gasped and fell back. He covered his eyes with his hand and blood streamed through his fingers.

The witch screamed with glee and spun away from us. Before our stunned eyes she melted into the shadows.

33

"Get her!" shouted Lucy, diving for the witch's legs.

Steve grabbed her cloak and yanked her back toward us while I flung myself on her, gagging as she hissed into my face. I held my breath and flung my arm around her neck.

Pain burned as her claws gouged at my eyes. But I kept my grip and Steve pinned her arms while I got her in a headlock.

"Careful," said Dad, wiping blood from his face with one hand while he took hold of the witch with the other. "She's an old lady. You don't want to hurt her. Here, let me take her. Lucy, go up and tell Mrs. Winter to call the police."

Lucy ran and the witch growled and spat as Dad dragged her, grunting with effort, toward the stairs.

Miss Everett twisted in the policemen's grasp and looked back at the house. "I'll get you," she shrieked as they wrestled her toward the waiting ambulance. "You can't stop me, I'll get you all!"

Dad followed them outside and she spat horrible curses at him, words I'd never even heard. Mom kept us inside and we watched from the window as the police had to put her in a canvas straitjacket and carry her out to the waiting van.

The witch swept her eyes over the house until she found me. I flinched back from the window but her burning gaze stayed fixed on me.

"Get ready to die!" she screamed. "You'll never have the ruby. It's mine! I'll kill you slow and painful, all of you, one by one. The little girl first!"

Her evil laughter rang out over the trees and through the house. "HAHAHAAAAHAHAHA-HAHAAAAEEEEEE . . ."

Even after the doors to the ambulance were slammed shut and the vehicle made its slow way down the drive and out of our lives, her laughter seemed to rattle in our bones.

Mom shuddered as she turned away from the window. "To think we had that living in the basement the whole time." Her eyes widened at the unspoken pictures forming in her mind and she shivered again.

"We'd better get the basement cleaned up before Sally comes home from her play group," said Mom. "Let's try to make this a normal house again, how about that?"

"Good idea," said Dad, coming inside.

"I'll help," I said, hoping I might still find some clue to the missing jewel.

"We'll help, too," said Lucy. "I can't believe the whole town thought she was dead all these years."

I felt my stomach climbing up into my throat as we looked into the old lady's hiding place. She'd stuck a narrow cot between the wall and a stack of boxes. Around it was piled what seemed like years of garbage and food wrappers. But no missing teddy bear. And no jewels.

Dad waded in with a garbage bag. As he disturbed the mess, the witch's rotten stink rose into our faces in powerful waves.

Steve gulped. "Uh, I think I hear my mom calling," he said in a strangled voice.

"Phew, me, too!" said Lucy, edging toward the stairs holding her nose.

After they left we all got to work, getting rid of every trace of the old witch.

"Your mother and I thought you had quite an appetite," Dad said, sweeping doughnut boxes and ham wrappings into a garbage bag. "But she must have been stealing food every night. No wonder you thought we had ghosts."

"It gives me the creeps to think of her having the run of the place while we slept," said Mom. "But at least now we know where all those mysterious noises came from, right, Jay?" She looked at me with a shaky smile.

Dad tied up the last garbage bag. "And now everything will be back to normal around here."

I grinned back at him. I didn't think this house could ever be normal. But with the wicked witch gone at least the bad stuff would be over forever.

34

When we emerged back upstairs I could feel a charge in the air. It was all around us. Like sparkles you couldn't see. Or the tiny shocks you can get from shuffling your feet on a rug and touching somebody.

I knew what it meant. We'd found the witch and now she was gone — but Bobby was still here.

Looking around at the quiet, dim rooms, Mom gave herself a little shake and smiled a lopsided smile. "Funny," she said, "now that it's all over I can barely stand to stay here. I can't get the picture of her roaming the halls out of my mind."

Suddenly she turned to Dad. "We're nearly done with our work here, Dave. What say we pack up and head home tomorrow?"

Dad looked startled at first, then he grinned. "Sure," he said. "I'll start on the office right now."

"I assume you have no objections, Jason?" asked Mom, lifting an eyebrow.

"No," I said, trying to sound enthusiastic. "I'll go get my stuff packed up." But I couldn't shake the feeling that we were abandoning Bobby, maybe just when he needed us most.

As I started for the stairs, Mom called me back.

"Your sister will be home soon," she said. "I don't want any talk about what happened here, okay?"

But I didn't have to say anything to Sally. When she came in the house she noticed the change in atmosphere immediately. Even the air seemed lighter, easier to breathe.

"Bobby's happy," Sally told anybody who would listen. "He likes us."

I felt a little chill every time she said that. I hated to think of Bobby left all alone here. But worse, I wasn't so sure he'd let us leave him.

With all the excitement, supper was late that night. Afterwards Dad played Go Fish with Sally while Mom cleaned up. He was trying to calm her down but it didn't work.

Then Mom came in and said it was time for bed. "We've had quite a day, but now it's time to relax," she said. "We all need a good night's sleep."

"Sure, Mom."

She nodded as if that was settled. "Now, Jay, would you please help me put your sister to bed?"

I sighed and walked Sally up to her room. She wasn't even slightly tired. "Bobby doesn't want to go to sleep," she confided to me. "Bobby wants to play."

Mom was right behind us. Shaking her head, she came into Sally's room.

"Bobby will just have to go to sleep," said Mom, tucking Sally in. "We have a long ride ahead of us tomorrow."

Afterward, she and Dad came to my room.

"What's bothering you, Jason?" asked Dad, coming right to the point. "You seem very subdued."

"It's the shock, right?" put in Mom. "Finding out that horrible old woman's been playing tricks on you all this time?"

"But what about Bobby?" I blurted. "Sally knew his name. How would she know the name of a dead boy unless he told her?"

Mom made a face. "Sally would have heard the old lady wandering around the house at night, muttering the little boy's name," she said. "She invented Bobby to explain it to herself."

"That's right," said Dad, nodding in agreement. "She may be a little kid, but her imagination is just as strong as yours, Jason. Strong enough to make you believe in ghosts."

He grinned and ruffled my hair. "The poor old lady was crazy. Naturally she wanted us out of her house. So she did her best to make the place seem haunted. After fifty-odd years here, she knew every inch and corner. Roving through the house at night, moving things around, banging on the pipes, cutting off the electricity, making spooky noises — she was the 'ghost.' "

I pretended to be convinced. When they were gone I told myself it didn't matter. We'd done everything we could. Now, we were going home and in a week Sally and I would both have forgotten Bobby.

My parents were sure right about one thing, I thought, stretching out on my bed. I was ready for a good night's sleep. I dozed off immediately.

I dreamed about pleasant, normal things. Sleepy things.

And then the broken grandfather clock chimed midnight.

35

I was sitting bolt upright the instant I woke up.
BONNNG!

My scalp prickled. I forgot to breathe.

It wasn't over. Bobby wasn't going to let go of us that easy.

I braced myself for the sound of running footsteps down the hall. But the footsteps didn't come.
BONNNNNG!

I heard faint whispering coming from the hallway but couldn't make out the words.

Finally I couldn't stand it any longer. I had to see what was happening. But just as I pushed off the covers, my bedroom door swung slowly open.

A glowing light appeared in the doorway.

Inside the light I could see, very faintly, the image of a small boy. Bobby.

"Jason," came a far-off voice out of the light, *"Jason, please save me."*

Then suddenly the mysterious light slipped

away. The ghost boy was gone and I was left alone in darkness.

BONNNNNG!

The clock sounded louder, more insistent. Something told me to hurry.

I jumped out of bed and ran to the door.

The hallway was dark but there was another ball of ghostly light in front of Sally's door. I could see shapes moving inside the light but I couldn't make out what they were.

My heart began to pound with a strange fear. Sally!

I ran toward the light but I couldn't seem to get any closer. It was blindingly bright.

Then I heard Sally's voice.

"No, Bobby," she cried. "No, don't!"

Her frightened voice was coming from inside the light!

"Sally!" I shouted. "Sally!"

It was as if my voice broke through some barrier. The images inside the light took solid shape and turned toward me.

Sally and Bobby stood there, held together by the shimmering glow. They were holding hands. In her other hand Sally clutched her favorite blanket, like she was still half-asleep. Little Bobby held a teddy bear.

Bobby's grip tightened on Sally's hand. He frowned. His little body tensed. He was getting ready to run — and take my sister with him.

"No, Bobby," I screamed, my heart slamming in my chest. I poured on a last burst of energy. I was almost there, almost touching them.

The ghostly light rose up off the floor. Bobby drifted up inside it — and so did Sally.

I leaped toward the light but it rose out of my reach. My hands passed through the glow and left trails of light. My fingers tingled.

Sally and Bobby were getting smaller and smaller, rising to the ceiling. He was going back to his ghostly world and taking my little sister with him — forever!

36

I dashed into Sally's room and grabbed a chair to stand on. I positioned it under the ball of light and climbed up. "Sally," I yelled, "grab my hand!"

But she didn't seem to hear. The light bobbed gently away from me. It was growing dimmer and smaller, taking my sister with it.

Then I heard Sally's voice again. "No, Bobby," she said firmly. "This isn't the right way. NO!"

She jerked her hand out of his grasp.

There was a loud POP! and Sally fell backward, out of the glowing bubble.

I lunged over the top of the chair to try and break her fall.

Sally's hand reached for mine. I pulled her toward me. It was like she was falling through soft clouds, slowly and gently. She drifted into my arms and managed to get both her hands around my neck before the spell broke.

The chair tottered.

WHAM!

I lost my balance and went crashing to the floor. The whole house shook.

Sally crawled off my chest, unhurt. "Jason, we have to help Bobby," she said urgently, her face all scrunched up with worry. She pulled at me. "Come on, get up. We have to hurry!"

It took me a couple seconds to get my wind back.

As I started to push myself off the floor, a door opened down the hall. It was Mom and Dad's door. I was almost relieved.

"What's going on out here?" Dad demanded. "Do you two know it's the middle of the night?"

Before I could answer, Mom appeared, too, tying her bathrobe belt. "We know you kids are still excited about — everything — but you really have to go back to bed and forget all about ghosts and — "

Mom stopped suddenly with a sharp intake of breath.

"What the — ?" breathed Dad.

They were staring wide-eyed at something behind me.

I turned.

Bobby was back. And my parents could see him.

37

The glowing light had faded a lot but it was still pretty impressive.

The shimmer clung to the outline of the small boy who stood looking at us from the other end of the hall. His eyes were big and sad. The rest of him wasn't very substantial. We could see right through him.

But the eyes. They made you want to cry just looking into them.

Then he was gone. Just like that, he winked out.

"Impossible!" whispered Dad.

"His eyes," breathed Mom. She grabbed Sally's hand and clutched it tight. "That poor child. He looked so sad. So very, very sad."

Nobody said anything else. It was like we all were waiting for what came next.

Then suddenly the attic door swung open by itself. A bright harsh light spilled out into the hallway, making everything look sharp and hard-edged.

"Hurry, Mom," urged Sally, yanking on her hand. "We have to help. Up in the attic, quick! That's Bobby's bedroom."

I figured my parents would never go for that. But much to my surprise Mom let Sally pull her along, and me and Dad followed.

I was scared but not as scared as I'd been other nights. I didn't know why all of a sudden Mom and Dad could see him, too, but it was great having them with us.

Somehow it seemed like this time everything might work out all right. If we didn't make any mistakes.

"Wait, Carol," said Dad as we got near the attic door. "Let me go first."

The three of us stopped and Dad went ahead.

When the harsh light fell on him it took all the color out of his skin so he looked gray. It was weird and unsettling to see him like that, but he waved to let us know he was okay.

Mom gasped. "You stay here," she said, hurrying after Dad.

But of course we didn't. Sally and I had seen worse things than light that made you look dead.

At the bottom of the stairs we looked up. The light made us squint, but we could see Bobby clearly. He was standing on the stairs, hugging his teddy bear and shouting defiantly.

"That's my mommy's ruby. Grandma gave it to her and you can't have it!"

"Give it to me, you little brat!" The unexpected voice cut right through us.

The voice was young but I recognized it anyway. It was the old witch — the way she sounded when she was the nanny. A voice trapped in the past!

Her voice gave me shivers, it was so cold and nasty. I was glad we couldn't see her.

"No," cried Bobby, clutching his teddy bear to his chest.

Then he screamed in fear and ran down the stairs.

It happened so fast we couldn't get out of the way.

But the terrified child ran right through us. He didn't even know we were there.

BONNNNG!

The grandfather clock struck!

38

Suddenly it came to me! I knew what I had to do!

"Hurry!" I shouted, scooping up Sally.

"Jason!" cried Mom. "What are you doing?"

"Come on!" I yelled over my shoulder. "No time to explain."

I raced down the hallway and hurried downstairs to the first floor, moving a little slower with Sally in my arms.

BONNNNG!

The clock struck again, louder than I'd ever heard it before. The sound echoed, bouncing off the walls and floors, making the whole house shake.

Suddenly there was a sharp CRACK! of lightning and I saw Mom and Dad frozen on the stairs. Thunder rolled over the house and a terrible wind rushed the house from all sides.

I pushed Sally under the stairs, afraid the windows might blow in again.

Mom and Dad came running down the stairs to join us. "Jason, what are you doing?" yelled Mom over the noise of the wind.

BONNNNG!

I shook my head, shushing her with my hand. I strained my ears. With the crash of the thunder, the howling wind, and the rattling windows I was afraid I wouldn't hear in time.

The clock struck again. The floor shook under our feet.

Then a grating voice pierced the air. *"Give it to me!"* shrieked the nanny. *"It's mine, all mine!"*

"No," screamed the little boy, sounding more terrified than defiant.

And then came the running footsteps. Footsteps hurtling down the hall as fast as they could go. Little steps, then big ones crashing after.

Lightning flashed through the house and thunder, shaking the walls. But the sound of the chase above our heads was more terrible.

"Oh, Jason, please help," cried Sally, hiding her face in her blanket. "Nobody ever tried to save poor Bobby. He's all alone!"

Suddenly there was a tug on my arm.

I was nearly jerked off my feet.

39

"Come on, Jason!" shouted Dad. "Carol, grab Sally! We've got to get out of here before this whole house comes crashing down on our heads!"

"No, Dad, wait!" I cried. But he was pulling me toward the door. If we left now it would never end, I knew it. Bobby would be stuck here forever — and part of us with him!

Besides, I wasn't at all sure Bobby would let us leave. Not all of us, anyway.

Not Sally.

"We'll discuss it outside," Dad insisted, keeping his grip on my arm.

Sally struggled to get away from Mom, then broke free just as we reached the front door.

Sally raced back to the stairs. "Bobby!" she cried. "I'll help!"

Trailing her blanket, she started up the stairs.

Horrified, I shook off Dad's hand and went after her.

Seeing me, she went faster. Above us Bobby's footsteps pounded. His thumping heart vibrated against the walls of the house.

I reached for Sally. She twisted to avoid me and tripped on the end of her blanket. I grabbed her with one hand and raced back down the stairs.

The walls wheezed in and out with each of Bobby's sobbing breaths. Floorboards cracked under the heavy tread of the nanny who was chasing him to his death.

"We've got to save Bobby," I shouted. "It's the only way!"

Mom and Dad stared at me white-faced.

"How can we?" cried Mom. "The poor little boy is already dead. We can't change that."

There was no time to explain.

The running footsteps were right overhead. A floorboard crunched as the nanny reached out to grab Bobby.

"Quick," I yelled. "Grab the blanket!"

40

Somehow they knew what I meant.

Between us we shook out Sally's blanket and each of us held an end, so it was like a safety net.

All around us the house creaked and groaned. Plaster fell from the ceiling in huge chunks. Pictures dropped off the walls. Lamps crashed to the floor.

But none of us moved. We stood our ground.

Bobby screamed. There was a sharp CRACK! as his small body crashed through the banister rail.

Then a piercing scream of terror as the body we couldn't see hurtled through the air headed right for us.

THUMP!

Something heavy but invisible landed square on the blanket.

The clock began to strike crazily but we held on for dear life.

I don't know how long we stood there, rooted to the spot. But all at once we became aware of the silence.

The storm was over. And Bobby was really gone.

Slowly we lowered the blanket to the floor.

I stiffened. Mom gasped. There was a small lump under the blanket when we put it down.

Quickly I lifted the blanket and looked underneath. With a shout of surprise I whipped the blanket away.

There was an old teddy bear lying on the floor. A brown teddy bear with a raggedy, mended ear.

Sally let out a cry of delight and swept the mangy bear into her arms. She looked at me with a big smile.

"We did it," she said. "We saved Bobby!"

Then something over my shoulder made her eyes go wide.

"Look!" cried Sally. "Look!"

My stomach churned as I whipped around.

And then a huge feeling of happiness, like a wave, washed right through me.

The living room mirror was glowing. Bobby looked out from the center of it, a smile of happiness on his face, his eyes lit up with joy. He was waving at us.

Behind him, deep in the light, were two figures running toward him. As they came closer we could see one was a man, one a woman, and both were dressed in outdated clothes.

For a second my heart lurched with doubt — could there be more people chasing poor little Bobby?

Then their faces came into view. They were the happiest faces I'd ever seen. Tears of joy streamed from the woman's eyes as she fell to her knees and embraced Bobby. The man hugged them both, laughing for joy — although we couldn't hear him.

"They must be Bobby's mom and dad," whispered my mother in awe, her own voice breaking.

The three ghostly images turned away from us. The parents each took one of Bobby's hands and they all began to walk away into the light.

Once or twice Bobby twisted around to smile at us again.

I had to blink hard to keep from crying myself.

As they disappeared into the light, the glow followed, fading away. But as the last of the light winked out we saw words burned into the surface of the mirror.

The words said:

THANK YOU AND GOOD-BYE.

Filled with peace, we stared into the mirror, all of us linking hands, unwilling to move and break the wonderful spell.

Then the phone jangled. We all jumped.

"Who on earth — " muttered Mom, heading for the door.

My nose wrinkled. A horrible stink was rushing into the room. The hairs on my neck prickled with dread.

The nightmare was starting all over again.

41

"What's that smell?" asked Dad, cocking his head and looking worried.

"It's the w — "

"Gasoline!" Dad exclaimed. "I smell gasoline."

Just then Mom came running in. Even in the dark I could see her face had gone ghostly white. I knew what she was going to say.

"That was the hospital," she told Dad in a stricken voice. "Miss Everett has escaped. Hours ago, they think. She may be on her way back here."

"HAAAHAHAHAHAHEEEHEEEHAAAA!"

For a few seconds we were rooted to the spot as the old lady's insane laughter stunned us, seeming to come from all directions at once.

Her evil voice came out of the darkness, gleefully taunting us, *"I told you I'd be back!"*

I whipped my head around but I couldn't tell where the voice was coming from.

Dad sniffed and then I smelled it, too: smoke!

"Quick," said Dad. "We've got to get out of here, now! Stay together."

He spread out his arms and shepherded us all through the dark toward the front door. The smell of burning wood grew stronger and Sally began to cough and choke on the rising smoke, hugging the mangy teddy bear to her chest.

It was hotter in the front hall. Dad stopped us. "Stay here until I get the front door open," he said, sounding strangely frightened.

Smoky sweat dripped into my eyes and stung.

Dad reached for the front doorknob. As he touched it, he let out a cry of pain, and at the same moment a tongue of flame darted from underneath the door and licked at his shoe.

There was a weird, quiet WHOOOSH! as if all the air was sucked out of the room, and suddenly the door exploded in flames, slamming us backward with a blast of fierce heat.

"Dave!" screamed Mom, darting right into the fire.

"Get back!" shouted Dad. "Head for the back door!"

But we couldn't move. He pushed Mom away and fell out of the fire, rolling on the floor. Flames were shooting up his arm. Mom whipped off her bathrobe and beat at the flames until they were out.

"Dave, are you all right?" cried Mom.

"I'm fine," he insisted. "Get going!"

140

Although his voice sounded strangled from the pain in his arm, he pushed us along the hallway. Behind us hot, orange light flickered, lighting our way.

Sally whimpered but none of us spoke. Dad's raspy breathing sounded as loud as the angry snap of the flames, as if he'd run a mile.

Nobody saw the wire the old witch had strung across the hall. I fell over it first, landing hard on my elbow with Sally tumbling on top of me. Mom caught her foot and twisted sideways to keep from toppling onto me and Sally. She landed with a piercing cry.

Dad ripped the wire out of the wall as Sally and I scrambled to our feet. But Mom was taking a long time getting up.

"My ankle," she whispered to Dad. "I think it's broken."

"All right," he said. "Grab hold of my shoulder and I'll lift you. Kids," he said sharply to me and Sally, "keep moving. Wait for us outside by the cherry tree. Move! Now!"

I grabbed Sally's hand and ran for the back door. It seemed a long ways away without Mom and Dad beside us. But there was no fire in the kitchen and the smoke smell seemed fainter.

I was afraid to touch the doorknob but I had to. Behind me I could hear Dad helping Mom along the hallway. I held my breath and reached for the doorknob. It was cool and turned easily.

Outside the night air was sweet and fresh. Sally and I breathed deep and waited for Mom and Dad.

"Come on, kids, get away from the house," said Dad as he came out, half-carrying Mom. "It might go up at any second."

He started down the slope ahead of us toward the cherry tree, Mom hopping and hobbling beside him.

"Let's go, Sally," I said, and reached for her hand.

But my fingers closed on air.

I spun around.

No Sally! She was gone!

Then I heard soft, vicious laughter from inside the house. *"You thought you'd escape me,"* whispered the evil old witch, sounding right beside my ear. *"But you won't get away. None of you will get away!"*

42

I darted back into the house, shouting over my shoulder for Dad. The witch stood in the kitchen doorway, Sally clutched tight against her. Behind them was the flickering glow of the fire at the front of the house.

"Daddy!" cried Sally. "Mommy!"

"You're all going to die," crooned the witch, backing slowly down the hall. Smoke drifted around her, making Sally cough.

In her white hospital gown, the evil old woman looked like a ghost. But the ghosts were gone, I thought, shaking so hard with fear I could barely move. There would be no Bobby to come to save us now.

"You thought you could steal my teddy bear," she hissed. Her wispy hair stood out from her head in patches and her fat white tongue roamed around her scrabby lips like a slug.

The witch took another step back. *"For years I searched and waited and searched. And you thought you could just come here and take it from me!"*

She grabbed at the teddy bear in Sally's arms but Sally clung tight and wouldn't let go.

"I'll teach you," growled the witch. *"I'll get you just like I got that other brat."*

"Bobby will save me," said Sally, hugging the moth-eaten teddy bear. She squirmed but the witch grinned, showing her blackened teeth, and clutched Sally tighter.

The air was thick and hard to breathe. "Let her go and you can have the teddy bear," I said, moving deeper into the house toward them.

She just laughed and plucked something out of her pocket. It was only when she flicked the end of the wooden match against her fingernail that I realized what it was.

And only then — too late — did I smell the gasoline all around me.

I dove, launching myself down the hall, and flinched from the tiny flame of the match as it sailed over my head.

WHOOOOOOSH!

There was a soft, deadly sound as all the air rushed away. I felt myself being sucked backward. I felt the white heat before I heard the explosion of fire.

"Jason!" screamed Sally from far away.

I couldn't breathe. My throat burned and my lungs felt full of needles. On hands and knees I crawled down the hall, feeling the fire leap higher behind me.

"Sally! Jason!" It was Dad, trying to get in. But the back door was a sheet of flame, the kitchen was full of fire.

We were trapped. There was no way out.

The old witch threw back her head and howled with glee.

Sally kicked with both feet and her heel connected with the old lady's knee. The witch let out a yelp and Sally punched her in the stomach.

For an instant her claws relaxed their grip. Sally squirmed and was free.

"Go, Sally," I yelled and started after her.

The witch leaped in front of me, her eyes fiercer than the fire. She's only an old lady, I reminded myself as I kept going. Then she snatched up something from off the floor — a gasoline can.

That stopped me.

"Your little sister won't be so pretty as a crispy critter, will she?" taunted the witch, swinging the can so that gasoline spattered the floor between us. *"She'll never escape me. I'll make a torch from her pretty blond hair. A blazing torch!"*

The witch swung the gasoline can again. This was it! I lashed out with my foot and caught the can squarely, knocking it out of her hand.

Shoving her with all my might, I pushed past and raced after Sally, calling her name.

Flames licked the wall. The front door was no

longer visible as the fire leaped high, nibbling at the ceiling. The smoke was so thick I could barely see my hand in front of my face.

"Sally!" I called.

"Jason!" Her voice sounded distant and I couldn't see her.

Beside me the grandfather clock made a sighing noise. Startled, I whipped around just as the old clock was engulfed in flames. The face still watched me but all its old menace was gone. Now it just looked surprised as it melted away.

As the clock wobbled and crashed to the floor the smoke parted and I finally caught sight of Sally.

She was surrounded by a ring of fire.

I called her name again but it was like she didn't hear me. She looked around wildly, her face white and her eyes big.

Then suddenly she ran right into the flames.

"Sally!"

I hurled myself through the fire after her, holding my arms over my head.

But she was gone. Choking on the smoke, I dodged a falling beam and fell.

As I looked up I saw Sally. She was on the stairs to the second floor, running up and still clutching that stupid teddy bear.

I called out in horror, knowing she couldn't hear me. The upstairs hall wasn't yet burning but I could see the glow of fire from the bedrooms. It was only a matter of minutes before the whole second floor went up in flames.

Scrambling to my feet, I rushed the stairs. Behind me somewhere deep in the house I heard my father calling.

I felt a leap of hope. "Dad!" I yelled. "Sally's upstairs!"

My eyes searched the smoke for a glimpse of him. But suddenly something huge shot out of the dark and bowled me off my feet.

There was a shriek of triumph and the witch shot past me and scuttled toward the stairway. I lunged after her, grabbing for the hem of her ghostly gown.

Missed!

The old lady seemed to fly up the stairs. I dashed after her. She snarled and turned on me. An instant too late I saw the gas can aimed at my head.

WHAM!

The world went black.

When I opened my eyes there was a sheet of flame between me and the top of the stairs.

I heard a shrill scream and looked up to see Sally running with all her might down the upstairs hall. The teddy bear dangled from one small hand. It was like she was Bobby, running for his life.

Behind her came the nanny, the witch!

"Give me my teddy bear!" she shrieked, her voice louder than the roar of the fire.

All around them flames danced along the walls and edged across the ceiling. Sparks fell to the floor and little fires sprang to life everywhere.

Sally ran faster, her terror growing.

I had to get to her. I scrambled to my feet and charged the flames in front of me. But the heat blasted me backward. It was so intense my skin felt blistered.

I looked up and Sally was still running. But the witch was gaining on her. I could see foam flying from her mouth.

My heart felt like it was bursting. I lowered my head to charge the fire again but the flames roared up at me, higher than ever.

"Give me my teddy bear!" screamed the witch. *"It's mine, MINE!"*

With a stab of horror I realized what was happening. Above me I heard Sally's little footsteps desperately running, the witch's gaining, always gaining.

Bobby was gone. Sally was going to take his place. Sally and the nanny would both die here and haunt this awful place forever.

"No!" I screamed, running once more at the fire.

But it was too late.

Sally hit the banister and with a loud crack it gave way. Her scream turned my heart to ice.

Her little body hurtled through the air, the flames leaping high to meet her.

And then —

"Jason!" Dad appeared out of the smoke, covered in soot. His voice was raspy and his clothes were singed. "Where's Sally?" asked Dad, panting with exhaustion.

Blinking away tears, I couldn't speak. I pointed with a shaky finger. Above us another section of the banister fell away, showering sparks everywhere.

Dad gasped and choked. While all around us the fire raged red and white hot, Sally floated above us in a cool blue bubble. Bobby was in the bubble with her and between them they were holding the teddy bear.

"NO!"

A mad scream pierced the air with such fury even the fire shivered. The witch stood against the banister, leaning out, shaking her fist at the bubble. *"You can't get away. You're mine."*

Her eyes were blazing coals and her mouth was a black hole flecked with foam. She lunged at the bubble.

The banister gave way and the witch teetered out over nothing. For an instant she swayed, still snarling. Then the fire leaped up and hugged her tight.

There was a loud CRACK and everything crashed in at once — the banister, the hallway, the ceiling, the floor. The witch. All of it went up in an explosion of flames.

But somehow we were still alive.

The house heaved a deep sigh as the roof fell, bounced, and settled to the ground for good. The house and everything that had happened here was finished. But for some reason I wasn't scared anymore.

Then I noticed I wasn't hot anymore, either. The blue bubble was floating toward us and the fire fell away from it. The bubble wrapped around us and we sailed out over the house down to the cherry tree.

43

"Are we all ready?" asked Mom, putting a fluttery hand to her lips as she cast one more horrified look at the steaming pile of ashes and rubble that used to be the house on Cherry Street.

We were all exhausted. Mom tenderly wiped a last smudge of soot off Sally's neck. We'd been up all night trying to explain things to the police and the fire department.

Dad did pretty well after the ambulance people bandaged up his arm. He didn't mention any ghost but he told them all about the witch, only he kept calling her Miss Everett. There were a few gaps in his telling of it but the sight of Dad with his hair all burned off and his bloodshot eyes seemed to account for that.

The only thing no one could figure was Sally. Mom's ankle was broken and Dad's arm was burned and I was going to look pretty funny for a while without any eyebrows. But Sally had come through the worst of the fire without even a singed lock of hair.

Her face and clothes were streaked with soot but even that was mostly from us hugging her afterwards. The police just shook their heads. I heard one of them say that parents can get pretty "overwrought" in a situation like that. It was obvious they didn't believe Sally had really been in danger.

Then the TV people came and things got really confusing. They kept pestering the cops about "Miss Everett" and trying to get pictures of us in front of the burning house. The police clammed up about the old witch and we didn't tell them anything, either.

But I couldn't help wondering. Her body still hadn't been found. I could see the firemen searching through the rubble but some of it was too hot for them to get to. Maybe she was in one of those places.

I hoped they would find her.

The sun was up by the time the police told us we could go. The ambulance people wanted to take Mom and Dad to the hospital but Mom said "no." All we wanted to do was go home.

We got into the station wagon and fastened our seat belts. Mom twisted around in her seat. "Sally, have you got Winky?" she asked. Mom's eyes had crinkles around them and she still looked scared.

Sally held up the stuffed bunny in one hand, Bobby's old teddy bear in the other. "Don't be sad, Mommy," she said. "Bobby's happy now."

Mom's eyes widened but all she said was, "That's good, honey. Try and get some rest, we'll be home in a couple of hours."

"And glad to be there, too," said Dad, turning the key in the ignition.

We rolled down the driveway and pulled out onto the road. I twisted around in the seat as we passed Steve's house to wave one last time to him and Lucy. I hoped I'd see them again — maybe even next summer — but not if we had to stay anywhere on Cherry Street.

Sally sang a little song to her stuffed animals as we drove on out to the highway. I settled back in my seat, thinking of all the stuff I'd do once we got home.

Then Sally made a weird noise. "*Jaayyyyyy-ssssoooon!*" she whispered in a gruff, raspy voice.

I shot up in my seat. But Bobby couldn't be here! Could he? Could he have decided he didn't want to leave my little sister after all?

I was afraid to look in Sally eyes. But I swallowed and made myself turn to her.

Sally giggled. Her blue eyes were clear and innocent, the eyes of a mischievous little girl.

"I was only fooling, Jason," she said. "But look what I found!"

She slipped her hand along the seam of the teddy bear's back. The seam parted. Sally reached in and brought out something big in her hand.

Sally opened her hand and showed me. It was a farewell present from Bobby. Glossy red and gleaming in the sunlight.

The ruby!

About the Authors

RODMAN PHILBRICK is the author of numerous mysteries and suspense stories for adults, and the much-acclaimed Young Adult novel *Freak the Mighty*. LYNN HARNETT is an award-winning journalist and a founding editor of *Kidwriters Monthly*. The husband-and-wife writing team divide their time between Kittery, Maine, and the Florida Keys.